More Praise for Paradise Dance

"A varied and accomplished debut collection from a longtime live storyteller. Solid work from a writer who should have been recognized long ago."
—*Kirkus Reviews*

"Mike Lee's stories provide a literary feast! They're gritty, but unafraid of the risks of sentiment, and leavened with wit. Here's a range of characters to delight in, all of them flawed, but courageously human. And his milieu, Albright, Massachusetts, a mill town in decline, is a world-in-small, one this reader came to know as if he had lived there himself. And the title story alone is worth the price of this collection. What a fine gathering of fictions, craft and heart and style—bravo!"
—Gordon Weaver, Author of *Circling Byzantium* and *The Way We Know in Dreams*

"I've always admired Lee for his fast ball. His breaking stuff never sucked either. But not until the publication of Paradise Dance did I get a look at his change-up. It's an education watching him work. And a thrill to see him throwing in the majors. To him and to all who have yet to read him: Welcome to the show."
—Robert Sabbag, Author of *Snowblind* and *Loaded: A Misadventure on the Marijuana Trail*

Paradise Dance

Paradise Dance

Stories by

Michael Lee

With An Introduction by
James Carroll

Leapfrog Press
Wellfleet, Massachusetts

Published in 2002 in the United States by
The Leapfrog Press
P.O. Box 1495
95 Commercial Street
Wellfleet, MA 02667-1495, USA
www.leapfrogpress.com

Printed in Canada

First Edition

10 9 8 7 6 5 4 3 2 1

Distributed in the United States by
Consortium Book Sales and Distribution
St. Paul, Minnesota 55114
www.cbsd.com

Library of Congress Cataloging-in-Publication Data

Lee, Michael
    Paradise dance : stories / by Michael Lee.— 1st ed.
        p. cm.
    ISBN 0-9679520-6-9
        1. Massachusetts—Social life and customs—Fiction. 2. Working
class families—Fiction. 3. Boston Region (Mass.)—Fiction. 4.
Working class—Fiction. I. Title.

PS3612.E345 P37 2002
813'.6—dc21

                                                          2002003294

Some stories in this collection had their first appearance in the following
publications:
The Yale Review: "The Albright Kid"
Temper: "Glory"
The Cape Cod Voice: "A Fresh Start"

For my mother, for her unconditional love and loyalty.
And in loving memory of my father.

"At the bottom of the heart of every human being from earliest infancy until the tomb, there is something that goes on indomitably expecting, in the teeth of all experience of crimes committed, suffered, and witnessed, that good and not evil will be done to him. It is this above all that is sacred in every human being."
—Simone Weil.

"Courage—fear that has said its prayers."
—Dorothy Bernard.

Contents

An Introduction to the Stories of Michael Lee

The town of Albright, Massachusetts takes its character from where it is—on the margins—and from what it was—a place built around a working mill. Now the mill is gone, and the world elsewhere has moved on. The people of Albright carry the weight of the past, with little sense of future. Paradise, to them, is the movie theater downtown, and it won't be long before the highway Cineplex does to it what time has done to the town.

The subjects of these unfailingly poignant stories are the people of Albright—waitresses, mechanics, small business owners, teachers, the mayor's son, vets, honky-tonk musicians, a little leaguer, guys with a great idea for a miniature golf course, town workers, the mayor's wife. A writing workshop, several bars, the shadows of Vietnam, the junkyard of wrecked marriages, Albright Hospital, the Albright Memorial Cemetery, the school, a weedy industrial park, and always, endlessly, the road—these are the places in which the stories unfold. Each one is entirely particular, rendering the experience of one or two people whom we have never met before, yet they are familiar. We know these people well, yet Lee has written them unlike any other writer. And what their places add up to—no paradise—is nothing less than the earth itself, which is more than enough. The geography of disappointment, too, can be a wonder.

Michael Lee's writing is inventive, strong, luminous, but his achievement in these stories goes beyond the rare clarity of voice and style that is their mark. His achievement is to have taken the mundane experience of ordinary human beings with absolute seriousness, and in doing so he lays bare—no, celebrates—the dignity and value that adhere in every life. In Lee's hands, the facts of failure, even of offense, open into the possibility of acceptance. This is so even for those characters who are trapped in time, the desperadoes and losers and brawlers who, because of the compassion with which Lee writes of them, seem not so different from the reader, safe in a chair. Because of Lee, in fact, the reader, for a while, becomes trapped in time, too—a confrontation through fiction with the hard truth of life, that, as they might say in Albright, *so aren't we all?*

What is eternity, Lee asks, but standing under a fly ball, driving to Taos, waiting for the ambulance, thinking of what to engrave on a tombstone, keeping a secret when there is none, regretting a marriage, asking for a date, hoping for the Red Sox? And what is the ordinary world when observed with feeling, wisdom, generosity, and, yes, love—if not paradise after all? Such is the precious, brave work of Michael Lee in this book. These stores open into eternity like that, and they faithfully render the earth—this one, ours—as the garden we wrongly think we lost.

—James Carroll
Boston, Massachusetts

Glory

"For rarely are sons similar to their fathers:
most are worse, and a few are better."
—Homer

MY FATHER came by ten minutes early in his customary fashion-lock from the 1950's, a janitorial splendor of pressed khakis, white socks and black crepe-soled shoes that yipped on my kitchen linoleum like cornered mice. He topped off the ensemble with a brown and yellow striped shirt, spread wide at the throat in order to display a sparkling white t-shirt. Ace's hair, finally all gray, was slicked straight back, the combed rows lining up like a planted field. All in all, he looked like the shiny hood ornament on a preserved old car.

You could kid Ace about how he dressed and combed his hair, but at 74 he was still a pretty good looking guy. I envied this since it had been my genetic blunder to inherit looks from Ma's side of the family – a hawk nosed, beady-eyed bunch of Yankee farmers with block heads settled on long gawky necks. On the women this gene softened to make them look mysteriously alluring, while the men, myself included, had to settle for appearing top heavy and vaguely guilty.

Ace shook a Lucky out of the pack and offered it to me. I waved it off and he lit up, snapping his Zippo over with a flick and slipping it into his pocket with the flair of a neighborhood magician.

"This is gonna suck, you know," I said to him.

"I hate that word suck. And it's not gonna suck. You're just going there to have a few beers with your old man. It ain't like you're joining a secret lodge or something. It's just the boys."

I sighed and grabbed my jacket, a cheesy tan thing that looked good for the first couple of days after K Mart.

"There's an example right there. The boys. Nobody calls people 'the boys' anymore. Makes you sound like Edward G. Robinson."

"So who calls their father Ace, hah?"

He had me there and we both smiled. I can't remember my brother Jake or me ever calling him "Dad" or "Pop." He was Ace to everyone, *especially* his sons.

In Albright, Massachusetts, like a lot of old New England mill towns, time was dusting its tracks, covering up guys like Ace and his pals. But it didn't seem that long ago when Jake and I were kids, laying in the dark safety of our bunk beds, whispering of the wondrous places we would go, always far away from Albright.

"I'm goin' to Borneo and shoot a tiger," I said to Jake.

"Tahiti, that's for me," Jake said from the top bunk. "It's warm all the time, nobody works, and the women walk around with their boobies bare."

"C'mon."

"I'm not kiddin', I saw it in a book. You can keep your smelly old Borneo, I'm goin' to Tahiti."

Neither one of us got to our destinations. Jake got closer, but it all ended for him in a sudden jangle when his patrol was ambushed just outside Khe Sanh on a January day in 1968 compressed by low clouds and a steady rain. He was walking point for an eight-man team when the jungle exploded in chaos and Jake was hit with a hot knurl of metal that bored into his left armpit, tumbling and slashing a frightful path to his young heart. Things have seemed much less important since that day.

When Ace and I got outside, I saw he had walked the mile and a half to my apartment. We got into my Toyota and drove off, all part of our new spend-more-time-together campaign. Ace was dragging me to the Frontier, an old watering hole located in downtown Albright in the basement of the Revere Hotel, a battered Victorian with twenty sad rooms and a myriad of hopeless stories. Our train station—the halfway point between Boston to the east and Worcester to the west—inspired the construction of the hotel back in the days when people got off to spend time in Albright. But soon enough we'll be a town outside the window, slowly clanging by.

I parked in the small lot of the Revere and we went seven steps below street level to the heavy metal door of the Frontier. Ace scraped the door open and inside the light from the television flickered over the dozen men at the bar. There was a faint smell of sour milk. Ace introduced me to a few of his friends, though we all recognized each other from daily installments of life in the same town. I was one of Ace's sons—the other one, maybe, but one nonetheless—and that was all I'd need in a place like this.

Henry Vaughan, the bartender since Ike was a lieutenant, plodded over to us. Ace held up two fingers and Henry nodded, bending down to frisk a couple Budweisers out of the beer cooler. He leaned over the beer chest for a good while, and a braid of blood vessel appeared on Henry's forehead like a rope of gray lightning until he finally surfaced with the beer.

Pretty soon I recognized an old high school classmate a few stools down, a lousy son of a bitch named Toby Valentine. He was gathered around a glass of beer and thumbing through the TV channels with the remote control. The other guys at the bar, all a generation older than Toby or me, blinked every time he changed the channel. Toby finally looked over and saw me.

"Hey. Bobby Dunne, right? What you up to these days, Dunne?"

"Nothing much," I said, "I'm sort of a computer jockey, working over at Middlesex Graphics in Sudbury."

I would have filled him in on the sparse details of my uncomplicated life—divorced a while ago, and now had one remarried wife and one perpetually angry adult daughter – but Toby wasn't interested in me 32 years ago, and not much has happened since. He had played a menacing role in high school and, if the arraignments and court reports printed in the *Albright Eagle* were accurate, had turned it into something of a lifestyle.

"You look like a mile run and a good cigar would kill you, Dunne," he said. "Hey, how 'bout you and me arm wrestle for beer? Or maybe money?"

Throughout my life I've always seemed to rub guys like Toby the wrong way—the arm wrestlers, the beer chuggers, the guys in the bleachers at Fenway. I ignored this latest challenge and turned back to speak to Ace. Toby flipped on the Bruins game just as the national anthem came on; then, from nowhere, his hand appeared and closed around my arm.

"A little respect for the anthem, huh?" Toby said. "You're talking right in the middle of the home of the brave. I'd think you of all people would show some more respect."

"Let's not touch tonight, huh, Toby?" I said, yanking my arm out from his grip. A sneer crooked the thin line of his mouth. Toby was shopping for a hard time and here I was, the first stop.

"You don't have much respect for nothin', do you, Dunne?"

I kept quiet, but the uneasy stir of conflict fluttered through me. "What's the problem, Toby?" I finally asked him.

"*Jay*-sus Christ, I come in here to watch a hockey game," Ace said, scowling at both of us, "and you two want to act it out. Toby, whyn't you go have a Dr. Pepper and play more a that pinball. You must be close to national champeen caliber by now."

"Your brother would have sat down with me in a New York minute," he said, ignoring Ace.

"And whipped your ass too," I reminded him.

"We won't know that now, will we?" he said, close enough to my face that I could smell his last Jim Beam and Marlboro.

I heard Ace's bar stool creak behind me and then he was between us.

"No more of that bullshit," he said to Toby quietly. "You want to run your mouth, we'll live with it, but no more about Jake."

I turned away and pretended to be interested in the game, but could have cared less about it. Toby didn't answer Ace, but got up on his own good time and strolled down the bar giving every couple of guys a little of his ragtime.

After we finished our beers, Ace said to me, "I have to be up early, let's pack it in."

I knew it was for my benefit. One of the few times I go out with Ace to a local joint and Toby had put an edge on it and made the evening seem pointless. Nobody drank at the Frontier for its ambiance, but no one came in here to be embarrassed either. I stood while Ace skimmed some dollar bills across the bar to old Henry. Then we were almost out of there, my hand on the door, when I turned back and stepped right out of character.

"Hey Toby," I yelled down across the bar, "You going to be here tomorrow night?"

I'm not sure what the compulsion was—certainly no manly code I believed in—but there I was, trying to be prickly, and every eye turned toward me. The din of conversation ebbed into quiet until the only sound was the reedy whine of the television.

"I'm here every night, Sweet Pea, whaddya want?"

I could feel Ace's eyes on my back and I said, "I want you and your arm on that table. Tomorrow night."

"Why not right now, Tiger?" Toby said, sliding off the stool with both arms raised.

"No, I want you to have a day to worry about it," I said, waving my hand in front of me. "I'll be here tomorrow night. Just make sure you are."

I stepped around Ace and yanked the door open, nearly whacking myself in the head with it. A medley of laughter trailed us up the steps. I knew Ace was angry with me and we sat in the car for a while not saying anything. The streetlight painted us in a dreamy luster and our clouded breaths gathered and rolled against the pitted windshield. When Ace finally spoke his voice came out wistfully, a tone you don't associate with him.

"You know, Toby's father Matt used to date your mother when we were all growing up. I'd see them on Saturday afternoons, lined up with half the town at the Paradise Theater to watch those Johnny Mack Brown movies."

I looked over at Ace. "I can't imagine old Matt Valentine with Ma," I said. But this filled me with a sense of wonder at the recovered moments of the lives of people you thought you knew better than yourself. And how it always forced you to reconstruct the script you carried in your heart. It occurred to me then, in a wave of shame, that I had depreciated my mother's life by thinking I knew everything about it.

"I don't know what you're trying to pull, but there's no sense in some damn fool game with Toby Valentine," Ace said. "You're not a gladiator for the Dunne family. There's no glory in this bullshit. It's just men hardened by time and their own dumb lives. I never should have brought you here, Bobby. You always had more sense than this. I guess most of what is old and left in this town is pissed off because they're old and left. Toby's no different, just a younger version. His boots are cold every morning when he yanks them on and then he *still* has to go out and grab a shovel. Believe me."

"So were yours, Ace."

"Yeah, every friggin' morning. But you're different. You're supposed to be smarter than all of us."

"Even Jake?" I blurted out.

Ace was quiet for a moment, then said, "Especially Jake. Dead might be brave, but it can't be smart, now, can it?"

It was the first time I ever heard Ace use the word dead in the same sentence with Jake. I didn't say anything more because I knew there were things that got ruined in this life that reason can never repair.

We pulled into Ace's driveway and up to the house where I'd spent my first 19 years—a sweep of time that nearly made up Jake's whole life. Even now, if it all ended for me at age 48 in the sudden tremble of a random moment, I would think my life had been much less than Jake's.

Ace said, "Come on in. Something I want to show you."

We walked into the living room, Ace heading for the liquor cabinet.

"You want one?" he asked over his shoulder.

"No, I'm all set," I said, collapsing onto the fold-down couch with the Revolutionary War slipcovers. The living room was unchanged since Ma's death four years ago and Ace kept it as meticulous as she had.

He rattled three fingers of Fleischmann's and ice around in the glass and sat next to me on the couch. Then he reached under the coffee table and dragged out one of the photo albums. The glossy intervals of our lives raced by as he fanned through the pages; Ace and Ma waving from a large blue DeSoto, Jake and me laughing on a ride at Paragon Park, Jake in the blue and gold Albright High football uniform. Jake had been a running back for the Bulldogs, a flashy player who slashed and danced through defensive lines of tough kids from Walpole and Brockton.

"Do you remember her?" Ace asked me. The flat paddle of his fingertip rested on a picture of Jake and a pretty blonde girl. They both looked impossibly young.

I shook my head. "Not really. Jake went out with a few of those. She looks like every blonde from the middle '60's." "Yeah, but this one was named Valerie and what was special about Val is that she was going out with Toby Valentine back in high school. Jake came down and plucked her right away from him like she was a baby bird. That poor shit Toby didn't know what hit him."

"Christ, that was a long time ago," I said.

"And maybe the most important thing that ever happened to Toby. Who knows?" Ace said. "Maybe he just wanted some get-back at your expense tonight, Bobby. I don't know. I'm just saying, might not have been too easy being a Valentine in this town all the time, either."

I looked at the photo. Jake was in his football jacket, smiling broadly at the camera, the number twenty-two on the sleeve. Valerie was pressed hard against him, her lips pursed as though the photo had been taken a second or two before she was ready. She *was* a looker.

"Whatever happened to her?" I asked.

Ace shook his head. "Who knows? It was just kid stuff with her and Jake. It didn't last a month."

"Can I have this picture?"

Ace hesitated, then scraped the plastic cover away and handed it to me. I got up to go and stopped at the front door.

"Maybe this is about you and Toby's father, too. I mean you taking Ma away from Matt Valentine and all."

Ace drained off the last of his whiskey, the ice rattling gently against his lip. "Could be that's what some of life is, cleaning up the scatter from other lives. But hell, I'm no expert on any of that."

When I got back to my apartment, I sat at the kitchen table with the photo and studied the familiar map of my brother's face. I traced it lightly with my finger, through his stubble haircut and down his strong jaw line, over to his twice-broken nose. Then I spun the picture around on the slick formica table top and watched Jake and Valerie's image twirl. Jake's smile was in the center of the photo as it spun and seemed moored in place, a rotating grin that looked sad as it turned over, then happy again as the photo spun. I reached into the drawer behind me and took out a pair of scissors, then slid the photo between the blades.

My big brother Jake, who knew all the secrets now.

I went through the next day marveling at the inexorable nature of impending malice, as if the whole day had been condensed to hasten my showdown with Toby at the Frontier. When I trudged down the steps and scuffed the metal door open a little after seven, the regulars were in place. Ace was there, too, and handed me a beer.

"Trying to help me carbo-load?" I asked.

"Let's just forget this nonsense and drink beer," Ace said. "We can even go to one of those brass and fern bars out on Route 9."

I gave my father a ragged smile and tipped the beer to my lips.

Ace sighed and said, "You have your mother's stubbornness. But look, I put ten bucks on you anyway. I figure Toby dug a half a ditch today just to keep us in beer."

Toby sauntered over then and stood a couple of feet away from me, rocking slightly for balance. He looked mean and drunk strong.

"Whaddaya know, Dunne? What's that boxin' dude say? 'Get ready to rummm-bull!' I've had a few just to make things more even."

I held my hands up in front of Toby's face and wriggled my fingers at him.

"Licensed," I said.

25

"Since when you need a license to pick your nose?"

That was pretty good—even I got a kick out of it—but a few guys at the bar really went overboard into hysterics. Humor had an easy audience at the Frontier and all these guys were afraid of Toby. He had his shirt sleeves rolled up high, shamelessly brandishing the swollen slabs of his biceps. If I had them, I would have, too.

I drained my beer and said to him, "I'll give you one chance to back out now and I'll never bring it up again."

I hoped for a better laugh than I got.

"I'll tell you what, Bobby," Toby said, moving much closer to my face than I cared for. "Tell you the truth, I never liked you. I'm going to toy with you, introduce you to some pain. After tonight, Ace'll have to sign your rent checks 'cuz your arm isn't going to work too good for a while. Ever hear an arm snap, Bobby? It's loud. When it's your arm, it's the loudest fuckin' sound in the world."

"You mind if I freshen before the kill?" I said, heading toward the john.

"Don't think pissin' on your hand gunna help you either, tough guy," Toby said.

Ace followed me in.

"You going to help me do everything?" I asked him, standing at the urinal.

"Look, let this dipshit put you down and we'll get out of here. This doesn't have to be more than it is, Bobby. For Christ sakes, stop antagonizing him. What are you gonna gain from all this?"

"Just what are you afraid of, Ace? That your son Bobby might lose, or that a Dunne might lose to a Valentine?"

I was immediately sorry I had blurted that out. I was scared, but it was needlessly cruel. Except for me, Ace had buried everyone he loved in this life and still faced the morning like it was a gift. I didn't need to apologize to him when he saw the look on my face. There are always things fathers and sons don't need to say to each other, which is good because they rarely know how anyway. He nodded and pushed the door open, going back into the bar without another word.

I came out a couple minutes later and Toby was poised at the table, his arm raised as if he had stumbled upon the first right answer of his life. I sat down and grabbed his hand, trying to be rough with him but he didn't seem to notice. Our hands closed tightly and I was stunned at the garnered strength I felt in Toby's grip. Fuck any signal, I heaved with everything I had. His arm moved slightly backward, then Toby cinched his shoulders and brought our hands upright. He pushed my arm over easily until it was poised at an odd angle and a rill of pain meandered past my elbow. Then he pulled us up again. He was in no rush and my arm went up and down at his whim while a toothachey throb began to pulse in my shoulder.

The men were gathered around our table, hollering for Toby to put an end to it. They seemed disappointed this was not more of a contest, but then so was I. When I looked over Toby's shoulder, I saw Ace standing above him, a grim look on his face. Toby said a funny thing to me then. He locked eyes with me as though we were the only two people in the room and said, "How is it on your own, Bobby? How is it out there?"

I held Toby's gaze and then felt his hand relax slightly as he re-gripped for what I knew was his big finale. My lips began to part then, gradually, like the big red curtains at the Paradise Theater for the feature presentation. His father and my mother. Jake and Valerie. Toby looked down at my mouth. My grin spread wider, then began to stretch like the grin of a crazy man. Toby couldn't take his eyes off me now.

There was something there for him in the theater of that smile, something finally revealed when my lips parted enough for him to see the picture of Jake and Valerie braced against my teeth—Jake smiling that cocky smile of his that fell between a leer and a grin and Valerie scrunching her lips happily as if expecting a sudden kiss.

I could feel Toby's grasp relax again as the recollection tore through him. I *owned* the rat bastard at that moment. Another victory for the Dunnes, this one from the most improbable. Just before I gathered whatever force I could to throw Toby's arm over, I shot a glance up at Ace. He appeared sad and tired now, as though something bad that had been put away was out again. And when I looked back at Toby, I wondered for the first time if my brother ever saw the face of the man who killed him.

It was there for me. Right there. They'd talk about this in the Frontier for the next two months. Imagine that—Bobby Dunne. It was a way of finally joining the old guard of a town that I knew then mattered little to me. What did matter to me was Ace, and in that fragment of time, when I saw the loss pooled in my father's eyes, it felt like Toby had his grip on my throat. Our sweet Jake. Poor all of us. What was it Ace said—how smart is dead?

I closed my mouth abruptly and that small motion was enough to snap Toby back. He looked at our hands locked together and quickly threw my arm onto the table. Then he let go and leaned back, but didn't look at me. I expected the worst, really, for Toby to fly off the chair and pummel me or turn on Ace. But he just sat there, his eyes trailing off toward the pinball machine. The barroom was quiet again and I casually put my hand to my mouth as though to wipe it off, slipping the trimmed photo out and into my coat pocket.

"You're a better man than I am, Toby," I said, and meant every damn word of it at that moment. I stood and scraped the legs of the chair across the tile floor. It made a high-pitched sound that seemed to startle everyone and slowly the men dispersed, drifting off in twos and threes toward the bar. Excitement like this didn't happen every night in here. Ace leaned over and placed a ten dollar bill on the table. He patted Toby on the shoulder twice, almost lovingly, then we turned and walked out of the gray maw of the Frontier, up the cement steps to the graveled parking lot where Ace hugged me quickly without speaking.

There always seemed to be an extra layer of cold around the railroad station in the winter, as if the chill started somewhere in those wooded buffer zones between the towns and by the time it came rolling into Albright with icy momentum, it was unforgiving. This was an easy night for sadness and our collars went up against the wind.

A Fresh Start

"Oh, lonesome's a bad place to get crowded into."
— Kenneth Patchen

THE CITY had been stilled by the first snow of the year, draping a white veil over the slates and shingles of the red brick buildings. A cold breeze off the Charles River made the lights dance in the trees and a muffled quiet spread down to the streets. On the Longfellow Bridge, heading to and from Cambridge, the taillights of the cars looked like a moving string of ornaments.

It was too much charm to ignore even for those who viewed the holidays as a wad of Visa receipts and a glut too much of spiced rum. But this time of year Boston was a city buoyed by the blithe spirits of its tenants—doors were held open longer, cabs pulled over when you wanted them to, and smiles were dispensed as freely as if launched from a Pez dispenser. Had it been summer, the Red Sox might have been winning.

But it was all lost on Vern Pond as he and several thousand subway patrons hurtled their way through the puzzle of tunnels under the city. He kept himself from ricocheting off other commuters with a hearty grip on the overhead strap. Pond looked across the car and saw someone had scrawled, "OneNeoEon" in broad marker pen on the door of the train. He contemplated that for a few moments and liked it's circular nature. He said it softly aloud. Holidays be fucked, he wished it was his neck that was in that overhead strap.

Vern was on his way to that unavoidable cocktail party, the one thrown at home. It would be an exact replica of the last gathering attended by virtually all the same people. The Hoovers would be there, certainly. They lived three houses

33

down, but Vern and his wife Brenda saw them maybe twice a year and always at their own parties. Vern suddenly realized that he'd never been inside the Hoover's house, though they'd all lived in the same neighborhood in Albright for fifteen years.

Aptly named, the Hoovers would hang around the buffet table and scoop hors d'oeuvres as though they were both rebounding from anorexia. By the third round of drinks, both Hoovers would sport at least one oil-stained atoll adorning their shirts and Larry Hoover would be harboring a thin line of grease under his lower lip.

Vern loved living out in Albright *because* of the commute. On this rocket ride through light and dark, Vern allowed himself the luxury of self-pity and it tasted like Zambuca out of the freezer—just kept getting colder and sweeter. By the time he'd get off the subway in Chestnut Hill and climb aboard the commuter rail to Albright, Vern would have the entire scenario of tonight played out in advance.

They shot out of the black hole of the tunnel, climbing into the city's gathering dusk. The sun winked from behind the museum and when Vern leaned down to glance out the window, he looked directly into the alert hazel eyes of a woman. He smiled apologetically, moving his head to look past her. The woman tried to accommodate him but moved her head in the same direction. Now they both laughed.

"Sorry," Vern said, straightening up.

The car stopped and he scanned the faces of several nations as they clambered on. Vern never got tired of looking at these young men and women, a newer version of himself, all filled with their own sense of hope and immortality. And none of them stayed on as long as the switch to the Albright train.

Vern knew as surely as he dangled from the strap that Brenda was just now wrapping a ribbon of raw bacon around a nugget of sea scallop, impaling both with a non-flammable toothpick. A maestro of the neighborhood party, Brenda always went the extra mile with details like naughty joke cocktail napkins and trays of assorted pickles and white onions, erotically arranged. It never failed to elicit a titter. For those who took a pass on the porno platter, she made intricate and time-consuming garnishes: pepper boats and carrot oars, celery sailors pitching on an avocado sea.

The evening prattle would not turn ugly until halfway through Brenda's third Glen Livet—no more Cutty Sark since Vern's last promotion. She would rattle the ice around in her drink, light a cigarette, then make that irritating popping sound after taking a drag, blasting two majestic columns of smoke out the barrels of her nose. It reminded Vern of quitting time at the old Albright paper mill when he was a kid selling papers out front to the homeward bound, first shift workers.

Since it was her party, decorum demanded it be Brenda launch the first salvo of the evening, usually a minor grouse about someone allowing his leaves to blow over onto the meticulous grounds of a fussy neighbor. Or tonight, perhaps the complaint would start with Eva and Fred Zauchin's Great Dane, a miserable dog the size of a small cathedral who took towering shits in everyone else's front yard. Like her napkins, Brenda ended all her sentences with exclamations.

"Yeah," she might say about another absent neighbor, "That's Burt Lewis for you. The kind of guy that forgets your birthday, but always remembers your age!"

This would kick off a wave of sniggers followed by a systematic maligning session on those neighbors not in attendance. Hal Foxworth's werewolf toupee, Dave Iafrate's constant whining about his angina, Lou Ann Deveraux's impending breast augmentation of which Brenda would say, "Jesus, I saw her bra on the clothes line the other day and I thought they were drying out a couple of bear traps!"

Out past the city now and the car began to thin out after

each stop. Vern settled onto a plastic seat and remembered how much he loved riding the MTA when he was a boy, finally old enough to be allowed into Boston on his own. It didn't matter where the trains were going when young Vern threw his quarter in and watched the city heave and clatter by. It was better than anything playing on screen at the Paradise Theater in downtown Albright. On the rare occasions when the train was empty, a driver might let him sit up front near the controls. Careening through the dark heart of the tunnels, Vern felt as though he was being hurtled through space.

"It's beyond me," a voice next to Vern said.

He had commuted long enough to ignore passengers who spoke aloud and knew eye contact was your biggest enemy. But there was no hint of your standard subway whacko in this sturdy and credible female voice, so Vern granted himself a glance and for the second time looked into the face of the same woman.

"Sorry?" Vern said.

"We don't know each other and you've been sorry twice now," she chuckled. "What I said was why would anyone bring a car into the city anymore? It's beyond me. It's a nightmare in there trying to park unless you pay through the nose at one of those awful garages."

Vern looked out the window as if checking on her theory by gauging the amount of traffic.

"Oh. Ah," he said, and then couldn't think of what else to add.

She looked to be in her mid-30's, close to a decade younger than Vern, and attractive in the subtle ways of well-groomed women who are comfortable with themselves. She seemed out of place on the train, but her mouth was kind and those hazel eyes forthright.

Vern found his brain. "I drove in here for seven years, I

know what you mean. A major pain. Parking tickets, broken antennas, that goddamned Denver Boot and then the tow truck bandits. All of it made me a nervous wreck. Then one day my car actually did get stolen and I remember what a strange sense of relief I had."

This was probably more information than the woman wanted, Vern thought, but they both chuckled politely and she tilted her face back toward the window. When she spoke, it was more to the fading city outside the glass than to Vern.

"The city is at its most beautiful after a first snow," she said. "It's the only fresh start we get all year."

Wouldn't that be hitting all six, Vern thought. A fresh start. To go home tonight and not find those snotty fakes, the Belforti's, hanging around the liquor table, eyeing the CD player and guessing the price of every doodad in the house. Or Katey Haggarty and her bovine-faced husband, Jerome, always insisting they bring their own music to other people's parties. They'd start everyone off with some Grover Washington or George Winston, then after draining their own lousy seven-dollar bottle of wine, they'd throw on a Kenny G and open Vern's bottle of Grey Goose. Elevator music to damn good vodka. What a waste.

Just once Vern would love to slip some Eric Dolphy into the CD player and watch the fear creep into everyone's face. Musical carnage to their ears. At some point in the evening Katey will stop the party and insist everyone listen to a bloopers tape where popular television actors say "shit" and "fuck" after blowing their lines. This invariably halts whatever feeble momentum the party has gathered.

"Well, Merry Christmas," Vern said suddenly to the woman, just to have something else to say. "I *do* hope you have a nice holiday."

She continued to stare out the window and appeared as

relaxed now as if sitting at home on her sofa. Maybe she owned a chunk of stock in the MTA, Vern thought, and rode it daily to demonstrate her eccentricity.

"When I was growing up," she said into the window, "we had a big hill in our back yard. All the kids would come over with sleds and toboggans and we'd stay out all day, sliding down the hill then turning around and walking right back up. We were a relentless army of little snow ants.

"But when that first snow *did* come, I'd get up early so I could be the first one on that clean sweep of hill. Every step I took made me feel daring and exceptional, as though I was the only person in the universe and not one foot had been set down before me."

She turned from the window and looked softly into Vern's eyes. "It was thrilling to seem that important."

Vern knew the problem was not a cocktail party with his fusty Albright neighbors. That was merely the symptom, Doctor. He sensed he was losing a grip on something that was quickly becoming irretrievable. And instead of alarm he felt only indifference. It was like watching his life get off at the wrong stop and caring barely enough to give it a wave goodbye. Vern Pond? He got off in Wellesley or Framingham. So long, Vern, have a nice new life.

Air kisses and gentle boasting. Sexual innuendoes and references to way back when. The swirl of plastic highball stirrers – the red ones with the knockers that Don "Big Mac" McDonald always made a point of licking grotesquely with his thick, gray submarine tongue. Vern remembered that he and Brenda had not slept together for two months.

"Such a wonderful time of year," the voice said.
Vern tried to stop himself from saying "Sorry?" again, but only partly succeeded. She started to snicker at him, then

they exchanged an honest and candid look as if some convention of propriety had been waived for the moment with no consequences. Vern had glancing moments of intimacy with strangers before, but he greatly appreciated the timing of this one. In that instant he would have given her anything she asked for. He might have been willing to die for her.

The subway stopped and more passengers clambered off, and the cold air spread through the car. He and the woman looked out the window past the street to a small park. A bleak arc of evergreens formed a semi-circle around an open area and the wind kicked up twirling funnels of light snow, teasing the ground in small feathery pirouettes.

The driver's head poked out of the compartment. "We got an accident on the tracks ahead of us," he said. "They're guessing it's going to be about a twenty-minute delay. And before anyone complains, please understand I'm not too damned happy about it, neither."

Vern stared out at the park. It looked like the set of an old black and white movie, empty and forgotten, the echoes of the film crew lost in the swirling, chilly air. He felt as though his life had become etched in the lower case.

A fresh start.

Vern stood suddenly and offered his hand to the woman.

"What if we got off and walked through that park?" he said, his hand still held out between them. "We could be the first ones. Look how clean and smooth it is. We'd be back on the train before it takes off."

Her indecision lasted a beat too long and made them both slightly uncomfortable. The moment had passed.

"Ah. Well. Thank you, but I don't think so," she said finally, and turned toward the window again, gathering her pocketbook to her chest.

Vern nodded. "I'm sorry," he said, but neither acknowledged yet another apology. "Would you mind giving me a holler if the driver says the train's about to start?"

"Of course," she said, looking up at him. "And I hope you understand."

"Of course I do," Vern said, though he didn't.

Vern stepped down from the car and walked slowly ahead. The rim of the city was hushed under its frosty quilt. He gathered his coat against the chill and stood in front of the park, rocking and squeaking in his wingtips. Even in the fading light, it looked as though the world had been carpeted white. He started forward, but sensing movement behind him, stopped and turned around.

"I get off in two stops," she said, struggling in her heels. "I'm going home to cook dinner for my family and I don't want to know your name." Then she reached out for his hand. "But I thought it might be nice to feel important again."

Vern was amazed by the feeling of life in that hand, a fragile pulse throbbing somewhere at the base of her finger. It reminded him of a small fish he saw once in an aquarium, suspended in the water and completely transparent, all its organs visible and working in sync like a tiny perfect machine.

"Don't worry," Vern said to her, "I probably would have lied about my name anyway."

They entered the park tentatively, plowing a short wave of whiteness ahead of them. Vern held the woman's hand lightly and they both looked directly ahead. They paused together for a moment, as if summing up the journey before them. And then they advanced, each step uncharted, bravely forward—these gallant explorers of the universe. These first people to a primitive and spotless world.

Koza Nights

"Every murderer is probably somebody's old friend."
—Agatha Christie

There was an aroma in Koza, an exotic pungency that floated over the city like a low cloud, a smoky, cooked smell of bottom fish or poached squid with red sea cucumber. The Okinawans called it *asa* or *mozuku* soup, the Americans soldiers called it shit-fish stew, but whatever label anyone affixed to it, its sad perfume hovered relentlessly over those loud crackling nights.

Life played out openly here in the streets and alleys, under foot bridges and behind buildings, over splintered scraps of lumber and jigsaw shards of glass. And in the humid frenzy of those Saturday nights in Koza, the air was thick with lust. The men—husbands, lovers, and boys—prowled the night like leopards and as the evenings wore on and the bottles of Tiger beer accumulated, their memories of home became less precise. Those who still had money in their pockets this late into the night swaggered with sexual confidence.

The smells and high pitched cries, the jostle of neon on the wet streets; glossy hair, tight dresses and husky whispers—it was all part of a forbidden equation that made those nights overrun with a scarlet pleasure.

Some of the Americans were fresh from boyhood and many would be dead before Christmas.

Bill Lacey shut one eye and tried to focus on Robertson.
"Hold still," he said.
"I ain't moved, Lacey. You the one all dragon-eyed. Eyes goin' round like pin balls."

Robertson tipped the bottle to his lips while *Mustang Sally* roiled from the jukebox. Lacey lurched forward onto the dance floor by himself, shuffling into a jerky arm and leg dance. A few of the girls came by pointing and laughing at Lacey, and the one with the silver butterfly in her hair tried to mimic him, kicking her feet up and shaking her ass.

Robertson drained the bottle. He had just enough beer in him to give the girls a halo around their gleaming hair and sweet powder faces. Lacey came back to the bar.

"Jesus, Robbie, sometimes you can just fuckin' taste life, you know? *Taste* it!" Lacey's angular face swooped in on him.

"Yeah, and I think you been tastin' too much of it, too, Lacey. What all that shit with the arms and legs? You white boys all dance spastic." Robertson mimicked him as though trying to take flight and the barmaid laughed.

Lacey waved for another round as two Kozan girls shimmied over and started dancing with them at the bar. The Kozan with Robertson began to hump his leg slowly, in time to The Righteous Brothers' *Unchained Melody*. They both allowed themselves to be dragged out onto the dance floor, but did more humping than dancing.

"You can always tell what time it is by the quality of dance you get," Lacey said over his shoulder to Robertson. "I'd say it's getting mighty late, Robbie."

They were a couple of grunts temporarily attached to Battalion Headquarters over in Kin Village, another improbable twosome joined by chance in the Marine Corps. Lacey was from upstate New York, wiry, with auburn country-western hair that was already thinning before his twentieth birthday. Robertson, from one of the half-dozen black families in Albright, Massachusetts, was nineteen as well, but taller by an inch and broader by a lot.

When they finally left the Bald Eagle Bar and made their way down Ichigo Street, it was after three in the morning. Lacey and Robertson quick-stepped toward the end of Ichigo where it met a thin graveled pathway that was called The Alley. The Alley was a hundred yards long and only remarkable because this was the final walk, the last gasp of Saturday night. The whores were in high gear in The Alley, cackling at the marines and yipping to each other in high pitched hoots. The first night Lacey and Robertson went into Koza they were thrilled with the amazing availability of all that was previously denied them in life. And this stretch was an extension of that, because when The Alley came to life, no one was too drunk and no request too extreme.

A door slammed as Lacey walked past it and angry shouting rattled through a thin wall of plywood. In the recess of another doorway, a young man in dress khakis and a Kozan girl were fused standing up, slowly rolling into each other. Lacey and Robertson walked to the end of The Alley and the glimmer from nearby Ichigo Street daubed the black sky with a rosy haze.

"Might be time to get back," Lacey said. "I've got to make formation tomorrow or Top'll have my one lonely stripe."

Robertson laughed. "Those stripes ain't gonna do you no fuckin' good, Lacey. The more stripes you be gettin', the sooner you be dead when we go to the big show."

"So how come you got two, hah?"

"I'm a corporal because I'm a dead-eye motherfuckin' shot, Lacey. I got my stripes on the rifle range, nowhere's else."

Lacey snorted. "That's bullshit. They don't give stripes just because—"

"*Ogenki des ka?* Whooo, big boy, I love you very much now."

They turned but could only see the bottom half of her legs, jutting out from a doorway. Further back up The Alley a bottle smashed and from another doorway Robertson could hear Marvin Gaye and Tammi Terrell singing, *Your Precious Love.*

"You got cigarette? Malbolo?" She wriggled her toes at them.

"Baby, I got it all," Robertson said. He stepped into the darkness and sat beside her, shaking a couple cigarettes out of his pack and lighting them both. Their hands collided briefly in the shadows when he handed her the cigarette.

"*Arigato,*" she said.

"*Do itashimashte,*" Robertson answered.

She trilled happily. "You speak Japan, hah? Black man talk Okinawa. That very funny."

Robertson eased his arm around her and they smoked in the darkness, Lacey only seeing their faces lit in an orange glint from the cigarettes.

"Robbie, I think I caught a love whiff," he said. "I'm goin' back to the Eagle while you two get married." He turned and walked back toward Ichigo. Just before turning off The Alley he heard Robertson laughing drunkenly at the night.

Robertson had orders to join Kilo Company, 3/26th Marines in two days when the entire battalion was to be shipped on LST's down to DaNang and eventually up to Khe Sanh, the ghostliest place on the planet. This was Robertson's last night out on Okinawa and it was just as well for him. He had grown tired of the rutty troughs and the corduroy alleys; the faces half lit by candles, the musky vapor of their bodies. He was tired of butterfly girls, and he was especially tired of having to find his women in The Alley. It was one of the few places on this fucked up rock where the girls would even look at a black man.

Back in the Bald Eagle, Lacey tried to brush away the advance of a bar girl but they were more persistent this time of night. Lacey had lucked out at the last minute and been assigned to the base headquarters back at Kin Village. The regular Unit Diary man was due to rotate and despite Lacey's MOS as a rifleman, he'd scored high enough on his clericals to rate a secondary MOS as an office pinky. Who would have thought it looking at Lacey? Base headquarters grabbed him until a real clerk rotated to Okinawa. It might help him

46

avoid a visit to Vietnam entirely, which suited Lacey who didn't have an ounce of hard charge in him.

The barmaid put a beer down and Lacey watched it run over the bottle and pool on the dark mahogany. A Kozan girl settled on the empty stool next to him and pressed her leg into his.

"How 'bout cigarette?" she asked, pointing toward the one Lacey had just fired up.

Lacey shook one from his pack and watched her light it with a Zippo, a cartoon of an angry eagle emblazoned on it.

"What's that say?" Lacey asked, pointing at the lighter.

"Say Aiybone. My name Michiko. You call me that."

"Airborne?"

"Aiybone. It's my husband. He Aiybone. He send money alla time. I hope he no die."

Lacey knew that at this hour in Koza everyone was lying but no one was kidding. He smiled at Michiko and wondered where the poor bastard was who once owned that lighter. They went out onto the dance floor and Lacey was surprised at how drunk he was. He lurched in her arms while The Four Seasons harmonized and he tried to reach down to knead Michiko's ass. She tossed off a laugh and settled into him where they just swayed now and ignored the music.

Robertson came through the door then, his eyes darting around the room. When he spotted Lacey, he moved frantically out onto the dance floor and grabbed him by the arm.

"Hey, what the fuck, Robbie? I'm dancin' here."

Robertson had a strange look on his face and even in his own personal fog, Lacey noticed it.

"Lacey, we got to go. Now," Robertson said.

Lacey sighed and gave Michiko a kiss on the forehead. "I'm sure your husband will be glad to know his wife's safe and workin' in Koza," he said to her, squeezing her hand.

Robertson was nowhere in sight on the street, so Lacey

walked down Ichigo past The Roundup and The Alamo – the Kozans had a passion for the American west and almost every bar in this section of Koza either had a saloon-style swinging door or a stripper in six guns—until he heard a loud hiss from a doorway.

"Lacey."

Robertson could barely fit in the opening without scrapping his shoulders on either side.

"What, five minutes and you're done with that girl?" Lacey said, "Takes me longer n' that to cook instant oatmeal. And why are you hissin' like a snake?"

Robertson began to cry. This was so preposterously out of character for the swaggering Robertson that all Lacey could do was stare at him and not say anything. Robertson wasn't the first person to cry at night in Koza and definitely not the last but it unnerved Lacey to see this and he felt a swell of fear gather in his stomach.

"There's trouble. Serious trouble," Robertson choked out.

Lacey rocked slightly on his feet and looked up and down the street. They were all in trouble of some sort, everyone out here, he thought.

"What happened?"

"The girl. The Kozan."

Robertson suddenly grabbed Lacey's sleeve and pulled him along. They came out onto Okane Street and doubled back over to Midorito where they found a passageway that brought them out into the middle of The Alley. Lacey kept his mouth shut and allowed himself be led to the door where he had left Robertson and the girl. He saw it was partially open. Robertson stepped in quickly and motioned for Lacey to follow.

Lacey felt his way along a damp plaster wall as they descended a short flight of stairs. At the bottom was a small open space and Lacey could barely make out shapes under the basement window. There was a mattress in the corner of the room and Lacey began to wonder if this wasn't some big practical joke Robertson was pulling. He changed his mind when he saw the girl sprawled on the floor next to the mattress. No one rested in that position.

"Robbie, what the fuck? Is she? . . ."

"Yes," he said quietly sobbing, "She's fuckin' dead as shit, man."

"Jesus Christ, how?"

"Lacey, it was like a fuckin' movie, man. A movie. Like I couldn't do nothing about it. I said something that pissed her off, then she pissed me off, called me a name – I don't even know what the fuck happened. I was drunk, man. Then from out of nowhere, I was at the top of the stairs, when she turned around and popped me," Robertson took a deep breath and went on, "Imagine, an Alley whore clipping a marine! Right on the lip, she got me, Lacey, a good one." Robertson brought his hand up to his lip to offer proof.

"Then it was like somethin' else took over. I whacked her one and she went ass up and started tumblin' down the stairs and . . . oh shit, Lacey, I think her neck or back or something broke. But she's dead as hell, man, what are we gonna do?"

Lacey took a step backward. "Whoa. Big word there, Robbie. We."

"Lacey, you gotta help me out here. I can't go to jail on this rock, how these people are. I'll wind up dead as her if I don't kill myself first. You know that Lacey."

Lacey wasn't sure he knew that or anything else about this night. He did know that this wasn't the place either of them should be right now. As if reading his mind, Robertson stepped over to Lacey and touched his arm.

"Look, the harbor's a block over. If she's found in The Alley, they'll know it was a marine. At least if she's in the harbor, she might drift over to Naha City or Tokyo Bay and nobody'll know what the fuck. But here it's just a matter of time 'til they tab us."

"You keep talking like I helped shove her down the stairs, Robbie. How could you let something like this happen to you?"

They heard a scraping sound by the basement window and hunkered down into the shadows holding their breaths. Nothing.

Robertson was silent for a moment longer, then said. "We can roll her in the mattress. No one's going to see us this time of night once we're out of The Alley," he said quietly.

The fear came back to Lacey now like the delayed pain of an unexpected blow. "Robbie, let the Marine Corps handle it. An accident's an accident."

"She got a fuckin' lump under her eye where I clipped her looks like a bone tryin' to pop through. Besides this ain't no military installation, Lacey. This is gook law here. This is Koza. Jesus, Lacey, please, man, it's my life! Stringing my black ass up ain't going to bring her back. We can do this, Lacey."

Robertson began crying softly again and in the closeness of the basement they shared with the dead girl, it sounded as though he was blowing small puffs of air out his mouth.

Loyalty was a funny thing in men, Lacey thought. Sometimes it came too quickly, more like a reflex than anything else. And then you're stuck for a long time with a decision that came as suddenly out of the air as a line drive jumps off the bat and surprises the third baseman. It's not that you intended to catch the ball but the hand sprung open in reflex and there it was.

He looked down at the twisted form of the Kozan girl and back at Robertson. And then, summoning an allegiance he knew was full of holes even as it was formed, Lacey let out a long sigh and bent down to grasp the Kozan girl's bare ankles.

•　•　•　•　•

Robertson went off a pick set by the new kid from the

mail room and launched his jump shot from the top of the key with two ticks left on the gym clock. He might have been 49 years old and the oldest player on the company team but he still shot the deadliest three, whether he co-owned the company or not. So when that final so-sweet, seams-turning-backward shot arched perfectly into air and began it's three point journey back to Earth, everyone on the Albright TechTronics team was stunned when it clanged off the rim and skidded out of bounds with the buzzer going off as an added insult. Robertson felt not only stunned, but cheated.

"Tough luck, Boss, I thought you canned it."

"Good look, Mr. R., it was a good look."

Robertson returned the requisite high fives, the last time he would allow such familiarity from employees until next September when the men's league started up again.

Later he stood under the hot sting of the shower, letting the water drill his back long after everyone else had dressed and gone home. He kept himself in shape, running five miles every other day. On the off days he still got his aerobic level up into the target zone by vigorously screwing his current mistress, a budding young model from Worcester named Jerri Ann.

Robertson had always been careful with his outside dalliances and never risked going after the few local offers he received in the course of his week. He was good looking, rich, well-connected, and despite an ego that could break a few tackles now and then, well-liked.

The rest of the time he was a devoted community and family man. In fact, the people of his hometown of Albright thought he was solid enough to make him Kiwanis Man of the Year three years ago after the voters of Albright tabbed him as a town councilman. When Mayor Duke Henderson handed him the plaque, he shook Robertson's hand and said, "We can always use more of your kind around here, Robinson."

It didn't take Robertson long to learn the ropes of Albright government—not the procedures or protocol, but the people—and within a year and a half, he had assembled a solid group of supporters if he decided to stay in government.

Robertson was the kind of man who made Albright feel good about cultural diversity. He made it easy. He didn't rankle. And now he would lead.

It was nearly 8 p.m. when Robertson brought his Mercedes to the beginning of downtown Albright at the junction of Main and Lexington. Though he had grown up here and had come home decorated after his Vietnam stint – it had been his bad luck to be at Khe Sanh during the Tet offensive and his great good luck to have survived it with two purple hearts and a bronze star—it was only after he got his engineering degree at Northeastern and co-founded Albright TechTronics with a classmate that he felt he truly belonged in his own home town.

Having money didn't hurt either. Robertson married Lisa Moulter, the WASP poster child of a daughter whose father owned the Albright Patriot Mall, and then moved into their wedding present, a 4,000 square foot home in the gated Dorsey Woods community of Albright—the only black man who didn't drive out of there by dusk.

Two daughters later, Robertson discovered a few of things about himself he never would have imagined: he was an excellent businessman, he loved being a father, and he thought he could do well in politics.

His thoughts were on his daughters as he turned onto Main and headed past the Paradise Theater. Arlene was 18 and headed for Miami on a tennis scholarship. Alicia was two years younger, had no athletic ability and didn't light it up in the academic department, either. Robertson's worries over Alicia were only minor, though, because he also believed no one as good looking as his daughter would have too difficult a time of it. He wondered what life would be like when both girls were gone and it would be just Lisa and he alone again. He could predict exactly what his wife would say at virtually any given moment now, and wasn't looking forward to the prospect of quiet nights in front of the gas logs.

And then one night recently at a function for the retiring Chief of Police, Mayor Henderson rested one of his ham hands on Robertson's shoulder and said, "You're a credit to your people, Richardson."

That turned out to be the last thing Duke said to him, because three nights later, he had a heart attack in a Northborough motel room with a red hair-rinsed cocktail waitress named Josephine. And while that was the end of the insufferable Henderson maxims, it spelled the real beginning of Phil Robertson's political career. He would run for mayor.

Given the encroaching darkness and a mind full of busy life, Robertson gave himself credit for seeing the man out of the corner of his eye. There was nothing special to notice—his back was to the street and he was looking in the window of Taggart's Flowers—but Robertson had been imagining that moment for so long, playing it over and over in his head, that before he cut the Mercedes into the right lane and grabbed a parking space a block away, he knew he had seen Bill Lacey staring at lilies through Taggart's window as though he were headed to a prom. The same corn cob persona, the whispy suggestion of skin and bones through the loose clothing, and now, in Robertson's rearview mirror, that gangly hitch as the man walked away from the window. It was Lacey, all right, certainly a different variation from the one Robertson remembered, but he was sure of it and now that it happened, it was a relief. He had been expecting it every day for the past 30 years.

He got out of the car and walked a half-block ahead of Lacey to the small Veteran's Park that served as a nightly meeting place for Albright's recalcitrant teens. Robertson sat on one of the wooden benches and remembered when he was growing up his mother telling him to stay away from the Vet's Park because the kids hanging out there were just "convicts in training."

Lacey finally appeared at the end of the block and walked slowly toward the park. Robertson didn't wave at him, but sensed he had been seen. Lacey gave no sign of recognition either, but continued to walk deliberately toward Robertson.

When he was ten feet away, he stopped and said, "Hello Robbie."

Robbie. No one called Robertson that. He was Phil Robertson—Phil, Philip, Boss, Mr. Robertson, Daddy, Honey, Oh Yes—but never Robbie. Only one person he knew would call him that and he knew on that awful night in Koza that he would hear it again. He sensed it whispering behind him when he played his daily number or when he bought a copy of *Ebony* just to irritate Tommy Pettigrew at the newsstand. He heard Lacey calling him Robbie when he pretended to listen to his wife's James Taylor CDs or when he washed his Mercedes with the rest of the suits on Saturday morning and then let it rip on the Mass Pike out to Worcester, and later when he breathed in the hollow of Jerri Ann's neck he thought he heard it, and the next day, when he purposely missed putts with his father-in-law. Robbie, indeed.

"So how you doin', Lacey?" Robertson said, as though they had spoken yesterday over coffee.

"About as well as most failures," Lacey said, just as casually. "You don't seem too surprised to see me, Robbie. I'm out for a walk in beautiful downtown Albright and here you are. I knew I'd run into you eventually. I hope you appreciate me not calling you at home."

"I don't appreciate you being in town at all," Robertson said. "But we're going to deal with it right now."

The years had been far less kind to Lacey. Most of his hair was long gone and the few colorless strands that tangled on the sides hung over his ears. Lacey had a face accustomed to disappointment and he looked like a man who was no stranger to reading his newspaper second hand.

"No threats now, none of that," Lacey said.

"What do you want with me, Lacey?" Robertson flicked a pine needle from the crease of his pants leg.

"Hey, Semper Fi, Robbie. Guy can't stop into town say hi to an old marine buddy? Some fuckin' pal you are."

Robertson stood quickly and Lacey flinched just enough to make Robertson smile. Lacey smiled, too, but there wasn't a lot of humor behind it.

"You know, Robbie, when I got back from Oki, I got off the plane in L.A. and didn't get further east than Alhambra for the next twenty years. That ain't too far. You ever been to Alhambra, Robbie? It's not our kind of town. But you, Robbie, look at you. Suit, tie, big fuckin' watch, shiny shoes."

"How much, Lacey?"

Lacey nodded. "That's always the question, ain't it? Not howya been? Not 'what happened to you on Okinawa, Lacey,' just how much. I'll bet that's how you do business. Right to the point, not fucking around. The best deal is one that's fair to both sides."

"How much?"

Lacey cleared his throat and announced, "$25,000."

Robertson chuckled. "You must be nuts, man. Twenty-five grand? For what? To keep some bum from telling a lie about me?"

"That's not very nice and you're a fuck for saying that," Lacey said. "I was sure your pal that night in Koza."

This wasn't chump change to Robertson, but if it served its purpose, worth it to the dime. But a little negotiation was always part of any deal. It wasn't the money that bothered Robertson, it was his absolute belief that this was only the first ticket to be punched on Lacey's gravy train, and the only surprise was that Lacey had taken this long and a continent to find him. But then he did look as though he had walked all the way.

Lacey said, "I'm not doin' anything I don't have to do, Robbie, I want you to know that. I don't like this much. Doesn't exactly make me feel great asking you. But let's face it, you're doin' better than good."

"Somehow this doesn't feel like a request, Lacey. A request is something like, 'Hey, old pal, I'm a little short, how about staking me to a grand until I get back on my feet.' Twenty-five grand is blackmail, and why should I believe this will be the only time?"

"Let's put it this way, we've trusted each other with a secret all these years, why stop now?" Lacey paused. "Besides, I don't like cold weather and I hate those fuckin' Red Sox. And I really don't want to hang around this hamburg town of yours the rest of my life. I got too much Alhambra in my blood now."

"How'd you know I was running for mayor?"

"You know, that's the beauty of our modern age, Robbie. I knew a woman who worked part time in a library over in San Gabriel and about five years ago I asked her if she could see newspapers on the computer. Because of you I used to go to the library three or four times a week after that, and she'd get me the *Albright Eagle* up there like it was a TV show. There was something about you at least once a week in there, and then when that big dude you had as mayor died and you announced you were running, I figured I'd better get out here before you became our first black president. Then I'd never get through the Secret Service."

Robertson didn't say anything and watched a couple of kids drift into the park, lighting cigarettes or God-knows. He turned back to Lacey.

"This meeting's over. One time, Lacey. You get the one hit off me and then you are gone. Do you have a car?"

"I'm mobile enough, why?"

"I'll meet you tomorrow night at a place out on Route 9 in Wellesley. Shoto Gardens, you know it?"

"Fuck no, I don't know it. You're the one who's running for mayor around here."

Robertson took another step toward Lacey. "We're not going to have a problem, you and me," he spit out. "We're just not, so let's stay on topic. Don't get me in a pissing contest, Lacey. And do not try to over-fuck me."

Robertson reached over slowly and grabbed two fingers worth of Lacey's shirt.

"Let's pretend this is a friendly negotiation, can we?" Lacey said, prying at Robertson's fingers to no avail. "Let's start by taking your hands off me. You always did like the rough stuff, didn't you, Slugger?"

Lacey stepped back after Robertson released him. "I see you're not in reunion mode. Sure, I'll meet you at this Shit Garden. What time?"

"Shoto Gardens. You can't miss it, big neon sign on the right about a half mile over the Wellesley line on Rt. 9, maybe twenty minutes from Albright. I'll meet you out back in the parking lot tomorrow night around ten."

Lacey shook his head. "Nope. Sorry, Robbie, but I'm not an out back kind of guy. I want to see you where there's lots of people. How about we meet inside at the bar and I'll bring you up to date on my fascinating life, starting with all the questioning I went through with both the battalion commander's office and the Koza police right after you went to Nam."

"You came through it didn't you?" Robertson asked.

"I guess you could say that. Yeah. I came through. I sure didn't give you up. They didn't even contact you in Nam, did they?"

Robertson was uncomfortable talking about this with Lacey. In fact, back then the C.O. had called him in after a patrol one afternoon and asked him if he knew anything about a girl being killed in Koza along that strip the marines called The Alley. All marines with a pass that night were being questioned. Robertson said he had no idea and by the end of the next week the North Vietnamese Army regulars had built up so much around Khe Sanh, everyone was too busy filling sandbags to worry about a dead Kozan. Once the Tet offensive hit, any talk of trouble in Okinawa was forgotten.

"The phones were busy at Khe Sanh, Lacey," Robertson said. "You might have heard about it."

"Yeah, I heard you came back with some extra salad on your chest. Whoopdefuckin'doo. But you know one thing I'm noticing, Robbie? You don't use that word *we* too much anymore. 'What *we* gonna do, Lacey? What'll *we* say, Lacey?' It sure was an important word to you a long time ago. You remember how important, Robbie?"

Robertson brushed firmly against Lacey as he headed out of the park towards his car. Behind him he heard the Marine Corp hymn being whistled out of tune.

Lacey had parked his old Pontiac bomber behind the Paradise Theater to walk through town, something he'd been doing for the past three days. If Robbie hadn't found him, he knew where to find Robbie. He had decided to wait a few days and rented a room in the Revere Hotel just off the park for twenty bucks a night, and even at that price, he'd be scrambling by the end of the week. Lacey had hoped things would be a little friendlier, but then Robertson was perfectly right—he was being blackmailed—and even if "some bum were telling lies," he knew Robertson couldn't afford to deny Lacey's story. Fuck Robertson, he could call the touch anything he wanted.

Lacey didn't do much the next day. He took his customary walk through Albright and wondered what it would be like to live there. It was a nice enough town, just big enough where he could be anonymous—except with his friend, the would-be mayor. But no, the northeast was just not him. Maybe go down to Florida where he could drink Margaritas by day and knock back a few cognacs at night. Smell that jasmine in the air and look at those young bodies. That would be it, then. Miami.

At 8:00 pm, Robertson pulled his wife's SUV into the parking lot of the Ten Screen Cineplex off Rt. 9 in Wellesley, across from Shoto Gardens. He parked amidst a cluster of cars in front of the theaters and walked quickly toward the adjacent parking lot. Robertson wondered how early Lacey would be. He figured him to cheat by maybe an hour at the most. Guys like Lacey were lazy. That's if he could find the restaurant at all. Robertson came out the south entrance and looked up at the moon. The stars seemed close enough to be personal.

He decided to wait for Lacey in the tree-lined strip of land behind the restaurant's kitchen. A large dumpster was at the edge of the tree line on the left, concealing him on that side. Robertson doubted Lacey would appreciate the irony in meeting behind a Japanese restaurant. He was willing to go either way with Lacey—hard or easy. Easy was the envelope with $5000 in his jacket pocket, a lot less than Lacey wanted but Robertson figured more than he'd ever had.

In the day and a half since Robertson agreed to Lacey's demand, he had decided the sum was too excessive. All Lacey had done was help roll the Kozan up and keep his mouth shut. It had been Robertson who'd had to carry that load to the harbor and then think about her every day of his life.

For Lacey's trouble Robertson figured five grand was

enough, and five grand would be the easy solution. A harder one was the 9mm Beretta with no serial number in his other pocket. Just another tragedy among the homeless if it came to that. Didn't one die out in North Albright a few weeks ago? This was the worst-case scenario, Robertson knew, and really, the gun was just an extra pair of balls. But he'd be goddamned if he was about to sacrifice everything he worked his ass off for just to keep Lacey in perpetual Marlboros and Budweisers. The gun might help him appeal to Lacey's sense of logic.

Around 8:30 that night, Lacey got up from the bed and walked over to the window of his room. He had been in hundreds of rooms like this. His view from the second floor of the Revere Motel was of the Albright train station and the back of a boarded-up five and dime. Lacey opened his battered canvas bag. It had the word *Magic* stenciled on the side and when he stole it nearly eight months ago from some jerk snoring loudly in a Denver bus station, he wondered if it might be full of magic tricks—disappearing rabbits and docile doves, colored handkerchiefs that you pulled out of your sleeve forever. Lacey had always liked magic acts, but when he first opened the bag and sorted through a few smelly shirts, the only magic he pulled out was a loaded .32 revolver.

While Robertson tried to stay warm in the trees, Lacey pulled into the parking lot of the Seven Eleven store a few hundred yards beyond the restaurant. He had gone to Shoto Gardens immediately after his meeting with Robertson so he would know what the area looked like. Much as he wanted twenty-five grand, he wanted to keep his ass intact to spend it. And he especially didn't like that strip of land with the scrawny trees behind the restaurant. Good night cover for an old ambushing marine. He would settle in there and wait for Robertson to show up.

As he walked into the trees, he caught a glimpse of the kitchen crew through a window, their white uniforms moving like ghosts through the steamy panes. Lacey had been in some tight spots behind buildings before, but never when he had the silent power of a gun in his hand. He moved forward quietly to find a good hiding spot, over there by the dumpster.

Robertson looked across the lot to the back of the restaurant. He could see the cooks moving past each other and he was thinking how nice and warm it must be in there with their chattering banter and the sizzle of the hot pans.

Suddenly Lacey was standing to his right, as though he had materialized from the bark of a tree. The gun leveled at Robertson looked like an open mouth saying, "Oh." Robertson was so surprised he let out an involuntary cry that startled Lacey enough to make him jump and grip the pistol tighter.

"Jesus Christ, don't move, Robbie." Lacey said loudly. Then he laughed nervously. "Damn, you hear people say that all the time on TV. Funny huh? This whole life is funny, ain't it? Hard, but funny, Robbie. Now, how're we gonna handle this?"

Robertson recovered his dignity. "We're going to start with you putting that fucking gun down. That's the last thing you'll need, I'm not here for trouble."

But Lacey liked the heft of the gun and his confidence rose enough to wave it casually, the barrel catching a glint of light from the restaurant. He stepped directly in front of Robertson, just out of arm's reach.

"I guess you're just in here to take a leak and you liked it so much you decided to hang out a while, huh, Robbie?"

"I wasn't going to jump your ass if that's what you mean, I just wanted to try and protect myself from exactly what's happening right now."

"Just give me the money and you won't see this gun or me ever again."

"I thought you wanted to do this in public. Let's go inside," Robertson said, gesturing toward the restaurant.

"Plans change, Robbie. You of all people should know that. Now I don't want to have a lot of conversation and I don't want to fuck around with you. And I ain't giving you the chance to put your hands on me. Give it."

Robertson brought his hands up slowly. "All right," he said. "I'm going in my pocket."

"Very slowly, Robbie. Let's keep this among friends."

But Lacey's reflexes were all mixed up in the building anticipation and pre-celebration of just *one* goddamned plan in his life that seemed to be actually working. Twenty-five grand would buy him a lot of paella in Miami.

When he reached for the envelope, Lacey saw Robertson's other hand flash out quickly with its own gun. Neither man fired.

"Oh shit, Robbie."

The two men closed now to within inches of each other, their guns dug into the stomach in front of them, and Lacey smelled peppermint on Robertson's breath, like the breath of the Kozan girls, always sweetly spiced no matter what vileness had occurred ten minutes ago.

Robertson's gun felt like it could press through to touch Lacey's spine and made Lacey stick his own gun deeper into Robertson.

"Well here we are, Lacey," Robertson grunted.

"Yeah, here we are, Robbie. The Halls of Montezuma. A couple of real assholes. Doesn't have to be like this. We can both back off of this."

Robertson stared hard into Lacey's eyes and felt good about the fear he saw.

"You know, Lacey, back in Koza that night, it didn't happen exactly the way I told you."

"She never fell down those stairs, did she?"

Robertson's pistol was beginning to make it difficult for Lacey to breathe. "Oh she fell down them, all right. I just don't think she knew it at the time."

"There ain't no insult worth that," Lacey said.

Robertson ignored him. "I still see that look too," he said. "Sometimes I see that same hitch in the eyes of a client when we first meet. Or I hear the briefest hesitation in a voice, the tiniest hint of misgiving in a handshake. Hey, I even see it in my father-in-law's face, when he thinks nobody knows what's in his head."

"God damn, everyone's a Kozan to you, ain't they Robbie?"

Robertson imagined shooting Lacey, the bullet tearing through his frail body like it was a bubble and shattering his spine on the way out.

Lacey wondered what would happen if he pulled the trigger and shot the future mayor of Albright. He'd guess at this range the .32 would cause a great deal of damage, but he was no expert on ordinance.

A cook from inside the restaurant turned the stove fans on and the louvered filters opened with a great blast of air. Both men flinched from the noise and glanced quickly at the restaurant, then back at each other. In that moment they both knew something else had entered into this convergence, something long ago unspoken between them, something that, as foolish as they knew it had become, as recklessly escalated the guns had made it, now had to be played out.

Lacey thought of the Kozan girl's small ankles and how feathery and blue they were in the low light shining through that small cellar window. He hadn't looked at her face— never did—but kept his eyes down on her feet and ankles, and he had come to know those parts of her like they were his own because the scene had played over and over in his mind.

Robertson's thoughts inexplicably raced to whether he should get Alicia some singing lessons, something to set her apart from being just another young knockout. When he became mayor, he'd have to crack down on her social life some and he knew that would be a problem.

The loud exhaust fans shuttled the aroma of the kitchen out across the parking lot, far enough to waft over the two men. It carried a once-forgotten aroma into the mix, sharp enough to break them out of their own thoughts and back to the immediate reality. Lacey and Robertson looked into each other's faces for a way out, but didn't find any.

These are the longest moments of life.

"Hey, Robbie," Lacey said, just before both men did what they thought best, "you believe people pay good money for that shit-fish stew?"

Wives, Lovers, Maximilian

"Men and women, women and men. It will never work."
—Erica Jong

WE WERE drinking beer and watching weddings, the four of us in the medieval city of Venlo, near the Dutch-German border; drinking beer at the outdoor café and watching weddings across the square at the old Town Hall, a massive gray stone structure with yawning wooden doors. A Gypsy band came by and began to finger their flutes and saw on violins, while a tall man with a bushy mustache wheezed a melody from his ocarina and a woman dressed in white danced with a goose.

She moved between the tables and chairs like a spinning angel, the mainsail of her skirt licking out at the necks of the patrons while the goose she held like a basket of fruit honked at them. The flash of her strong thighs made me shift in my chair.

I reached for my glass and smiled first at Claire sitting across from me, then at her husband and my boss, the professor of modern Dutch literature, Josef Bergen. Next to me, my date Brenda kept time to the music with an annoying foot tap on the table leg that sent ripples through our beer.

"Josef," I asked, "don't you find it ironic that you Dutch are so private about your lives, but so public about your weddings?" I threw a two-and-a-half guilder coin into one of the Gypsy's baskets, vainly trying to catch the eye of the dancer.

"No, but I have come to believe we are an ironic culture," Bergen said to me. "You know, Reggie, as you become older, you get to loan out some of that irony to you younger folks."

An archetypal Bergenian comment: self-effacing, shaded with humor, and purposely vague.

"I couldn't imagine Josef and me walking up those stairs in front of the world," Claire said, smiling. The sun caught her small overbite in a gleam. "Him with his shoes scuffling and me with my gown sweeping the steps. Our wedding was far more private."

A bride and a groom came out of the large double doors of the great stone building and stood on the small balcony that overlooked the square. Applause broke out from the wedding guests gathered below, and a few sentimental drinkers from our café clapped as well. When the camera shutters clicked softly throughout the crowd, the sound echoed off the buildings that enclosed the square, sounding like a tisking of tongues.

Josef smiled at my date. "So, Brenda, you are new here? What do you think of my country, are we as filled with idiosyncrasy as Reggie implies?"

Brenda crinkled her nose, a signal that thought was taking place. It wasn't quite the smoking chimney at the Vatican, but there it was. She was in the homestretch of her third large draft, matching me pint for pint. Through the clear glass table I could see her red-tipped toes wriggling in their sandals. She leaned over to give Josef yet another view down her scoop neck jersey and the venerable professor, a true Dutchman, availed himself without disguise or shame. At twenty-five, Brenda was celebrating the salad days of her sensuality and was not uncomfortable with attention. I glanced quickly at Claire, but she was busy watching the next group of married couples climb the stairs to the town hall.

Claire Bergen was my age, mid-thirties, some twenty-five years younger than Josef. She was pleasant on the eyes and strongly constructed, the way Courbet would paint a woman, plentiful and robust, with the flesh applied lustily in gobs from a palette knife. Although as American as high crime, she was always mistaken for a sturdy Dutch wife.

"What I love about your country is the transportation system," Brenda said to Josef. "It's so efficient. And the trains are so, um, phallic? Charging into those dark tunnels. Very romantic, don't you think, Reggie?"

I'd learned to roll with Brenda's metaphors and withheld my opinion on the eroticism of the Dutch railroad. Instead, I cocked my empty glass in the waiter's direction. Josef chuckled softly into his napkin as though he couldn't get enough of these uncensored Americans.

"It's the law in Holland, you know," Claire said, lighting Josef's cigarette. "Everyone has to go before the magistrate in their town hall and get married before they can have a church ceremony. Day like today, I'll bet we'll see ten, fifteen weddings."

Josef let the smoke dribble out his nose. "This 'town hall,' as you call it, is old enough to have seen the marriage of Mary of Burgundy and Emperor Maximilian of Austria."

Whoever the hell they were.

"You and Joe get married here, too?" Brenda asked, and I wondered if that was the first time in his sixty-three years Dr. Bergen had been called 'Joe.' He seemed delighted.

"Claire and I and went to Germany to get married," Josef said, smiling at Brenda. "You know the holy city of Kevalar? It is just not far from here, perhaps thirty kilometers?"

Brenda rummaged through the files of her memory. "Isn't that the place Jesus Christ appeared in a bowl of chips or something? Some kind of stigma."

"Stigmata, Brenda," I said. "And it wasn't a bowl of chips, it was on the wall of a church."

Brenda gave me a nasty look. "Oh stigma, stigmata, smegma," she said, "It still doesn't make sense. You can't tell me God hasn't appeared in everything from tortillas to tip trays. If you were God would you act that way?"

"You *are* very refreshing," Josef said, in the Dutch tradition of summing you up to your face without insult. "And Reggie,

69

you have your facts wrong. It is only a stigmata if it bleeds from the wounds of Christ. The hands and feet and side."

Brenda inspected the palms of her hands and I accepted Josef's correction silently. It was Josef Bergen who had given me a job at the university in Maastricht despite my lackluster career as a mid-list novelist. Three books: a collection of hasty short stories and two novels, one of which had some good scenes, snappy dialogue, and should have been set in the old west.

Josef either didn't hear about or chose to ignore the unfortunate incident with a naïve coed at Hartwick College in Oneonta, New York, the scene of my last teaching job. I might have stayed there forever in upstate New York, what with their dark-paneled country bars and winding motorcycle roads, but I was one pressed charge away from a medium-sized scandal and the administration left little doubt who they would back in that mess.

At Maastricht I taught composition and short story writing to a variety of international students, all writing in English, all trying not to sound too international. The pay wasn't great, but good enough to keep up with my habits and two small rooms in the old city. It felt good to be anonymous for a while and not worry every time the phone rang.

And to thank Josef for all the kindnesses he'd shown me, I'd been sleeping with his wife Claire once a week for the past two months. In fact, Claire and I had been meeting in Kevalar, the very same holy city of the stigmata and her marriage. It had been Claire's idea to go to Germany for our liaisons and I always wondered if her adapting so much to Dutch life made our infidelity less grievous by taking it out of The Netherlands.

A gust of wind bullied through the crowded café, launching postcards, napkins, and a few pieces of lettuce that weren't weighted down by dressing. I had been shaky about this meeting, though it was nothing more than a social gesture, but things were not going well with Claire and me. Problems with guilt, I suspected—hers, of course. I had made friends with that demon a long time ago. But I thought it might be a good idea to demonstrate some boisterous heterosexuality with Brenda in front of Josef. And perhaps even Claire would become a little jealous. Brenda and I were only casual friends and last call lovers, but I thought if Josef had any suspicions, Brenda was the ticket. Very complicated adult stuff, all this.

"Reggie told me you write books, too, Joe," Brenda said. This straightened me in my chair because when Brenda and I had discussed this luncheon, I hadn't exactly given Josef's work glowing reviews. Stiff and stuffy were a couple of words I had floated out there.

Josef acknowledged our literary kinship with a wave of his hand. "Reggie's the writer," he said, "I'm a scholar who writes."

"Nonsense," Claire said. "Josef's last anthology was translated into Japanese."

Brenda laughed. "Whatever for?" she asked, inserting a black olive in her mouth and cradling it with her lips to form a red and black O.

"Will you excuse me?" Josef said, breaking the silence. He stood and rocked slightly on his feet, a pint and half of Gulpener Bock under his vest.

"Are you going to pee?" Brenda asked. "'Cuz if you are, I'll go, too."

Applause gathered in the square and clattered over to us. Another wedding party waved from the balcony of the town hall. Brenda and Josef linked arms and headed into the café. I squared around to look at Claire, but she was staring without expression at the wedding party. The sun bathed her peach face, lighting the tiny white hairs on her cheek. I lingered on the sunlit intimacy before speaking.

"This is working out OK, the four of us. Don't you think?" I asked.

She looked at me then and it wasn't the expression one expects from a lover, but I've sure seen it several times in my life. The whole afternoon could have ended right there, not another word spoken, and with that one look, I'd know Claire was trying to find the right words to put an end to us.

"Anything wrong, Claire?"

"This isn't the time, Reg, not now. Not here and especially not with us all half in the bag. This was a dumb idea right from the beginning. It feels as though you're threatening me with my husband. And then there's Brenda, a very sweet kid, but how could anyone so clothed be so naked? Exactly what role is she filling here?"

"Forget Brenda," I said, easing my hand over the table in the direction of her arm. "She serves a purpose for us."

Claire shook her head disgustedly, drawing her arm away, and lit a cigarette from Josef's pack. She blew the smoke over her head and it corkscrewed in the wind, spinning away from us.

"It occurs to me *everyone* serves a fucking purpose for you, Reggie."

"You know that's not true, how could you say that?"

"You have this uncanny knack for reminding me what a shit I am. Me, who's survived the lunacy of enough men to know better. My biggest disappointment is that I knew early on I could never fall in love with you. That ruined any pleasure that could come out of the danger of it."

The truth was I'd heard that before as well, with some variations. Maybe I'm just a bad guy.

"What if I say something to Josef about us? Would you deny it?" I asked.

Claire stabbed her cigarette out angrily in the ash tray. "You would, too, wouldn't you? And you wouldn't care what it did to him because it would serve your purpose."

"Look, I would never say anything to him. But you didn't seem to have Josef in mind when your ankles were up around your ears in Kevalar last Thursday if I recall correctly."

She whacked me a pretty good one and I have to say, for a woman on the verge of middle-aged amplitude, she had a quick left slap. It wasn't so much the force of it as its crispness. Another Gypsy came by just then and rattled his basket in my face.

"Beat it," I snapped at him. I wouldn't give Claire the satisfaction of rubbing my face, the left side of which was tingling in the sun. "You've been a willing participant all along, Claire."

She frowned. "Leave it to a writer, even a mediocre one like you, to come up with the exact word. A *participant* indeed."

Though I'd suspected for a couple of weeks that Claire was headed here, now that it came true, I was shocked to feel hollow and frightened. I'm usually on the other side of these matters; the one doing the backstep. But here in this square, where all the fresh promises seemed to bounce off the old stones, the weariness of my own life slumped against me. I wanted to be mad, but couldn't muster the effort until the waiter arrived and spilled the heads off our four pints onto his small tray.

"Watch what the hell you're doin', will ya, Cosmo?" I barked, then turned back to Claire. The sun glared down on us, but I didn't have that steel-balled confidence good beer can give you on a hot day. "This is just some passing guilt you have," I said. "What we have is. . . ."

Cheering rumbled across the square as an Indian couple smiled and waved to the crowd below the balcony. Claire glanced nervously toward the inside of the café. I was hoping Josef had Brenda leaned over a sink by now, giving her one for old Maximilian.

"I'll never be able to make it up to Josef," she said, "but I'm going to make it up to myself. I've been a goddamn fool with you, Reggie, but at least it was with you and not for you. Somehow that distinction seems more palatable." Claire stood up. "When Josef gets back, please tell him I decided to wait for him at the car. You can tell him I've had all the love and marriage I can stand for one afternoon,"

I stood and held my hands out to her, but couldn't think of anything to say.

"Or you can tell him anything you want, Reg. Anything you think may be appropriate for a participant."

"Claire, please." I finally managed to say, but hated the weakness in my voice, the desperate whine of the word *please*. Claire looked as though she had tasted something vile in the back of her throat and I knew that taste was me. Goddamnit, what did she know about living in rooms that stank from the last guy? She's never dozed off under pictures cut from calendars, dangling on a wall from a thin strip of tape like the scrapbook of a long lost family.

I stood quickly, banging my chair into the person behind me. He said something but I silenced him with a nasty look. Claire looked over her shoulder at me, her lips set tightly, forming a thin line that accented the parentheses at the corners of her mouth. I wondered if learning the Dutch language had somehow altered the set of her smile. I watched her walk away and even if I could have found my voice at that moment, I knew it would only be railing against a tide. I sat back down.

Josef and Brenda came back a few minutes later. I had finished my beer and was halfway through Claire's. For a moment I let the tip of my tongue rest on the rim of Claire's glass. Brenda's face scrunched up and it looked like, "Hey, where's Claire?" was coming out next. I put the beer down and got up and grabbed her by the arm, yanking her away from Josef and the table. Maximilian, my rosy red ass.

"Hey, take it easy!" Brenda said, but I had her locked in a desperate grip. We got cursed at in three or four different languages for bumping a few tables. When we finally made our way out into the open square, Brenda tripped on the cobblestones. She wobbled at the end of my arm and kept yelling something at me, but I wasn't having any of her shit, either. We must have cut a fine path because all the future brides and grooms parted for us as if I were Moses returning with some new rules. We got to the steps leading up to the landing of the town hall where a clog of people from the Indian wedding party still milled around.

When I fell over the bride's long dress, Brenda wrenched free. The commotion seemed to escalate quickly then, and a dark man in a tux came at me with bad intentions.

I took the stairs two at a time, shoving people out of the way until I was on the small balcony. I looked triumphantly across the square to the café. The Gypsy girl had stopped dancing and the goose had quit honking. My eyes wandered through the rubble of faces, all halted in conversation and turned towards the town hall, fascinated by this lurid scene I had caused and now heightened by my appearance on the balcony. The waiters and tourists, even those very private Dutch, stopped talking about their damned gardens and looked across the square. It almost seemed as though everyone was waiting for me to say something profound.

But it was Josef I could see most clearly—his gray mane, his small direct eyes, his library face. Josef slowly brought himself to his feet and reached down to the table picking up his pint of beer. And with that suffocating dignity of his, he raised his glass to me in toast. We locked eyes across the square and held them for a few moments, then I heard the rushing of footsteps coming up after me, the sound of my life about to take a sharp left turn yet again. Charges and explanations, angry words and incredulous glances; all too familiar ground.

I suppose the trick is to realize something from each bad turn of the wheel. I wasn't good at that. But now, as I looked at Josef in that final instant, something stirred in me that felt like acquired wisdom. I became calm and just kept looking at Josef. Even as four hands grappled with my arms, pinning them to my sides, I kept my eyes on Josef and then learned of the power even a terrible knowledge grants the man who knows how to wield it.

The Secrets
of
Cooperstown

"We dance round in a ring and suppose,
but the Secret sits in the middle and knows."
—Robert Frost

PESSIMISM ARRIVES cold and early in the December foothills of the Catskills and as Ray Blake turned onto I-88, he felt as though his body temperature had dropped a few degrees as well. The ride had been just as icy inside the car since a half hour out of Albright, Massachusetts when his wife, Pearl, had thrown a nutty only Ray seemed capable of igniting. Sometimes all it took was a gesture or a sigh, and lately—he swore it was true—a bad thought. This time it was Ray's mysterious insistence that they visit Cooperstown over the long Columbus Day weekend.

Pearl was always after him to get out of Albright on weekends. A month after her miscarriage five years ago, they tried their first sojourn and went to Cape Cod in October, walking the dunes and swamp trails in Wellfleet during the day and drinking slow bottles of wine at night in the restaurants along Commercial Street in Provincetown. It should have been a perfect healing weekend, but they both knew it was too soon once they crossed the Sagamore Bridge and had the entire peninsula of Cape Cod laid out before them. Neither of them was ready for the exclusive company of the other and it ended badly, with Ray skulking off to a bar in Wellfleet one afternoon and returning drunk with the notion of moving there and raising oysters.

There were other attempts at post-miscarriage bonding. A trip to New York City was somewhat successful due to the sheer volume of activities, but a long weekend splurge in Bermuda proved disastrous with petty flair-ups, and culminated in Pearl accidentally running into Ray with her motor scooter, breaking his pinky finger. Shit indeed happens but, to Ray's thinking, Pearl might have tried to squelch her laughter as he lay in a pile, twitching beneath a young cedar tree with his little finger pointing towards Newfoundland.

It wasn't until Ray insisted Pearl pack for their weekend in Cooperstown that he finally admitted to this Army re-union. Pearl couldn't have been more flabbergasted if Ray had tried to re-enlist.

"Cooperstown, for Christ's sakes, Ray," Pearl had said. "You haven't said more than boo about the Army in all the time I've known you, and now this reunion comes up and all of a sudden, your middle name is Rambo and it's the most important thing in the world? Honestly."

Now the relentless hum from the macadam filled the car as they rambled on in silence, and Ray cinched his grip on the Camaro's steering wheel for the umpteenth time. This Camaro, for example: her idea. A kid's car, for Christ sakes, and if that wasn't bad enough, she had it painted throbbing red. Ray felt as if he were driving his blood pressure around.

But Pearl had been right, it was completely out of character for Ray to want to go to something like this and aside from a few alcohol-inspired mutterings over the years, he'd been virtually close-lipped about his time in the Army or Vietnam.

She flicked at a peeling cuticle with the nail of her little finger. Pearl always kept that nail longer than the others and used it for the day-to-day picking, prying, and extraction chores that befall humanity. It was one of those idiosyncrasies that at the beginning of their marriage seemed so impossibly cute, so individualistic, an Asian affectation. Now Ray merely thought of that finger as Swiss Army Pearl.

Ray Blake was 53, hair either falling out or becoming a non-color, quite in sync with the encroaching paunch he felt slowly padding his midsection, a legacy handed down to him—instead of money or land—by his father and grandfather.

Pearl, on the other hand, was usually blond and nine years younger than Ray. She had married him when he first joined the history department at Massachusetts Bay Community College, where she was enrolled to get out of Albright and avoid waitressing for life with her girlfriends at Stumpy's Hamburgers, inevitably raising a lair of brooding, easily-infected children with an angry pickup-driver named Bucky, Chucky, or Gil.

Pearl knew her Albright men well and didn't want any of them. Within a few years of marriage it became apparent to Pearl that Ray might know the exact date of the Charge of the Light Brigade, but didn't have a clue how to advance himself through the ranks of the faculty at the college. And in a cruel slap of irony, Ray accepted a transfer to the Framingham campus of Mass Bay and they moved into a small house in Albright.

People talk, especially in the back-stabbing cavort of academia and Ray was just an average teacher—a fate worse than failure but loaded with company. When you are a relatively young and pretty wife of a stalled faculty member, as Pearl soon became, some of the men and two of the wives weren't afraid to make a friendly pass at you.

"Could they hold this reunion in a more remote spot?" Pearl asked as they passed yet another collapsed barn and leaning silo.

Ray agreed. "I think upstate New York is New Hampshire with Yankee caps and a few more teeth," he said. "Say, maybe we could go visit the Hall of Fame while we're there."

The suggestion was greeted with silence. A half hour off I-88, Ray throttled the Camaro down for a landing and took a right at the top of Main Street in Cooperstown, as sure a Main Street, USA as if you were on your way to the soda fountain to meet Veronica and Jughead for a root beer float.

"Take a left here," Pearl said and Ray obeyed instinctively, digging the Camaro's right wheels into the road. "When you get down to the end of the street, take another left, then pull into the big brick hotel. I want to show you something."

When they got out of the car, Pearl took Ray lightly by the arm and they walked over a spongy carpet of fallen leaves to the back of the hotel.

"This is the Otesaga veranda," Pearl said after they climbed the steps to a sweeping white porch. Past a spread of fallen leaves and fading lawn was a large palette of indigo that was Lake Otsego.

"And that, of course is the lake," Pearl said. "You know about Natty Bumppo and all that?"

Ray turned his collar up against the knifing breeze off the water. "I'm a history professor," he said. "That doesn't excuse me from reading literature."

"Oh I don't know that I'd call James Fenimore Cooper literature," Pearl said, surprising her husband with such an unPearl-like remark.

This was as close to repartee as they had managed in several months. Ray held off questioning her about her familiarity with the place, but soon realized he would be far more uncomfortable not knowing than not asking.

"I'm not about to defend James Fenimore Cooper," Ray said. "And just how *do* you know so much about this place?"

The utility fingernail flashed out like a stiletto and Pearl pried a shard of paint from the wooden railing. "I was here for a weekend with a friend before I met you. We stayed here and I remembered how beautiful the veranda was. Just thought I'd share it with you."

"How was the food?" Ray asked, looking out at the lake.

"Excuse me?"

"The food. You stayed here, how was the food?"

"Very funny," she said. "Now I've got a question for you. Why are we really here? What's up with this Army business?"

And in this way, more silence was brought to the foothills as though in homage to the setting sun. Two hours later,

Pearl perched on the arm of the couch in their Best Western motel room, running up and down the TV clicker like piano scales.

"Does this tie go OK with the shirt?" Ray asked.

Pearl looked up from the TV. "Yes," she said. "And so should we unless you want to be late."

"You know, I've been thinking about this and if you want to stay here or go somewhere else on your own tonight, I'd understand."

Pearl looked at Ray. When he dressed up, as he was to-night, he still had a bit of dash in him and she felt a brief fluttering of sadness run through her.

"You've never even heard from any of these guys all these years, have you?"

"No," Ray admitted. "But it's something I need to do."

"Then I'll go, too. Let's make an appearance and then try to salvage something out of this weekend, OK?"

Members of Ray's outfit, a unit of the 1st brigade, 9th infantry, were to meet for dinner at the Tunnicliff Inn, a two hundred year old hotel and watering hole in the middle of Cooperstown. Pearl had, in fact, become moon-howling drunk in the basement bar of the Tunnicliff on her weekend excursion years ago. And now, as though in the grip of some whirlpool, they climbed down the steps and into that very same bar known appropriately as "The Pit."

When Ray opened the door to let Pearl through, the energy of a packed room in full swing washed over them. Ray scanned the crowd quickly, but didn't recognize anyone right away.

A tall man with a silly handlebar moustache approached them.

"You folks here for the reunion?"

He looked vaguely familiar to Ray.

"We are," Ray said. "I'm Ray Blake, this is my wife Pearl."

Ray saw something pass over the man's face, perhaps a

glimmer of recognition, but he didn't introduce himself and merely stepped back to let them through.

"Bad attitude," Pearl muttered to Ray, "must have been an officer."

At the bar, Ray ordered them two Dewars rocks and met the glances of the men who were standing nearby.

"You gotta be shittin' me," he overheard one guy say. "I think it is."

Ray and Pearl found a small corner table and sat facing the crowd. Ray immediately saw that he had fared better than most. There were some guys in there that looked like his father, and Ray did especially well in the attractive wife department, which is another way men have of assessing each other.

"These people don't even seem to know you," she said to Ray as they sat alone. "You going to mingle?"

Ray sipped the remnants of his drink and waved at the waitress for two more. "Thirty years is a long time," he said, looking into the crowd.

"I don't know. This is a weird vibe. You sure this isn't a Korean reunion? We got the right war here, Ray?"

Ray let the remark pass but gave Pearl a look that brought another round of silence along with the scotch. They sat for twenty minutes more without anyone approaching their table and finally the smoky throng began its slow, noisy departure upstairs for the dinner. Pearl excused herself to join the long line at the ladies room.

The woman in front of her in line made Pearl laugh when she said, "I swear if we could get some toy tanks and trucks, these guys would sit on the floor and play until the beer ran out."

And then, as Pearl approached the door to the bathroom, the man with the handlebar moustache stopped at her side.

"Is that Ray Blake you're with?" he said. He looked like an old sepia photograph with those waxed ends to his moustache curling toward the ceiling.

Pearl stared back at him and finally said, "You heard his name when we came in the door. What's this all about?"

Another man, shorter and twice as wide, quickly appeared at his friend's side.

"Whaddya say, Lester, time to strap on the old feed bag?" He clapped Lester on the shoulder, obviously trying to steer him away from Pearl. "C'mon Lester, that was a lifetime ago," he said quietly. "We're all here for a good time now."

"We ain't all here, Richie," Lester said to the man. "Pokie and Reuben and Frank—I don't see them, do you? But I see shaky Blakey. I see him."

"Let's let it ride, Les," the man said, tugging at him now.

"Shaky Blakey," Lester repeated, looking at Pearl.

Pearl matched Lester's gaze and said, "If you've got something to say about my husband, I'd think you'd at least have the guts to say it to his face."

The one named Richie raised his eyebrows over that and Lester was silenced for a moment.

"Guts is an interesting word you used," he said. "Look, I don't mean you no disrespect, Ma'am, and I've had a bit to drink, I'll admit that. But your husband cost us some friends a long time ago and while some people are nicer about it than I am, like Richie here...".

Richie stepped forward and stuck out his hand. "Richie D'Orfino, Mrs. Blake. How'd ja do?"

Pearl took the fat man's hand and shook it up and down once.

"Anyway," Lester continued, "he turned and ran and left some good men behind. He even did it with a goddamn radio on his back. You can't do that, Ma'am." Lester was practically whining now. "All these years we've been doing this, he never showed up and now he's here and when some guys find out about it, they're going to rip him a new one. Much as I hate him, I'm suggesting you get him out of here right now. He dishonors us all by showing up."

Pearl could feel the heat rise into her scalp and she reeled against the lattice wall, her pulse pounding in her head. But even as she struggled with this new revelation about her husband, she immediately wondered if Ray knew how some of these men felt. And if he did have an inkling, why would he ever have come here?

She ignored her straining bladder and headed back to their table, watching her husband from across the room. He sat alone, idly playing with his glass and occasionally looking around, but his isolation was more pronounced now that she understood what some in the room must have felt.

"I'm not doing well at all here," she said as soon as she got back to the table. "And I want to go back to the room. Right now, no discussions, please. Please do this for me."

Pearl grabbed her coat and headed for the door, not waiting for any response. Ray quickly finished his drink and downed Pearl's as well. Outside the air had turned from crisp to cruel and they walked to the car bathed in a bright moon.

"Where don't you feel well?" Ray asked, putting his arm lightly around her shoulders.

"Everywhere," Pearl said.

They headed to the motel out on Route 80, Ray trying to make small talk on the road that ran parallel to the lake, but Pearl couldn't hold her water any better than a conversation and asked Ray to pull over. She got out and walked down a small embankment cast in a glimmering pewter from the moon, then squatted, holding on to a scrawny oak for balance. It felt endless, this urine gushing out of her, and she wished she could piss this terrible night away. These past five years away, too. Nothing felt right about this trip from the beginning. Nothing felt right, period. And that's when she heard a rustling sound several feet away in the underbrush followed by a great gasping of air.

"Ray!" she called out, frightened. "Ray down here!"

She could hear him scramble from the car and skid down

the embankment in his street shoes.

"What is it?" Ray said breathlessly.

Pearl had finally finished and stood, smoothing her skirt down and backing towards him. She pointed toward the underbrush. "Over there," she said. "Something over there."

They didn't move toward the sound, but stared into the tangled maze of brush until they could make out the struggling form of a large animal, its hind legs kicking out helplessly while it tried to right itself.

"Jesus, God, that's horrible," Pearl said.

Ray took a tentative step towards the underbrush and saw it was a deer. "Probably got hit by a car," he said. "I imagine it happens all the time out here."

After a slight hesitation, Ray stepped forward, parting the tangle of vines and limbs that weren't already flattened by the deer, and knelt by its head.

"Be careful, Ray, for Christ's sake."

But Ray didn't answer, and Pearl willed her feet forward so that she could see both her husband and the deer cast in an eerie shimmer as much from the lake now as the moon. The deer's breath came in short, frantic bursts and they could hear something clogged within the animal's air passage that made its breathing a great effort.

Pearl knelt across from her husband and then watched Ray, her bumbling, aging history professor, her failed husband, this freshly defined coward and the father of their dead child, pick the deer's head off the ground and cradled it in his lap, stroking it lightly. As all three of them exhaled out in short gasps, their breaths mingled into a burgeoning cloud that rose above the brush, hanging over them like a wispy powder for an instant, then broke apart and drifted out over the cold waters of the lake.

The struggle was over soon, and the only sounds of breathing came from Ray and Pearl. They sat a bit longer, looking at each other, then Ray got up, lowering the deer's head gently onto the ground and putting his arm around Pearl who had begun to weep softly into her hand. He helped her up the embankment and within five minutes, wheeled the Camaro to the parking spot in front of their motel room. He kept his hands on the steering wheel and stared through the windshield. Pearl's sobbing had stopped and the smell of the deer from Ray's clothing gave off a rusty pungency inside the car.

"I want you to go inside," Ray finally said. "I have to go back to the reunion."

Pearl searched for Ray's hand.

"No you don't. Ray, don't do this. Baby, come inside with me."

He turned fully in his seat towards her and in that light from the motel and the moon, Pearl thought her husband looked like he did when they first met—young and confident, a man with a clean blotter and full of the time-released strength this life would demand. It seemed as though all their years together quickly passed in time again like some sobering review. They sat in the car and the only sound between them was the crackling and sizzle of the motel's neon street sign.

Pearl leaned into him finally, kissing him lightly on the lips, then squeezed his hand gently before sliding out of the car. She'd try to watch some TV in bed, maybe, but that always made her sleepy. The same for reading. They used to joke about how Pearl reserved the bed for just a couple of worthwhile activities. One thing she knew for sure, though: she was determined to wait up for her husband, no matter how long it took.

Territorial Rights

"A place belongs forever to whoever claims it hardest."
—Joan Didion

AS SOON as we walk into the joint, I smell trouble, because you don't have to be Mr. Spock to know when you're out of place. It's been like that all along for Frankie and me, ever since we left Albright and some fourteen hours later hit the first Stuckey's where we wolfed down our pecan pies and kept heading south.

A couple days, several gin joints, and ten points lower on our IQ's, we've stopped in some podunk one-horser in Oklahoma to quench more of that thirst. The bar we're in is one of those low-ceilinged dives where all the smoke and lies are swimming around two feet above your head. Most of the women in here have big cakey hair and lots of face paint, and then you got Merle Haggard or some other shit whining out of the jukebox. Musicians like Frankie and me—well, Frankie's a drummer, so technically, he's not a musician—are supposed to be able to relate to all kinds of music, but that country western stuff leaves me chilly. All that drawly fussing about his woman going away with some tall me-hoff truck driver and taking his faithful three-legged dog with him. Get over it, buddy.

I look over at Frankie who's just as out of place as me, but looks a little more so. Frankie's small and whatcha call wiry, which means he's got a nose that's been broken and a bad attitude. All these towns have been the same for three nights now, pitching and rolling through them in Frankie's '89 Bonneville. Fifty-five bucks of gas a day and I'm wondering if we'll have anything left once we get to Taos, which is our goal, getting to Taos, New Mexico. Not that anything great is waiting for us there, just that Frankie has an ex-brother-in-law who teaches pottery to senior citizens and we might have a place to stay. Won't he be surprised to see us wheel in?

The bartender comes over to us like he drew the short straw. I've been hearing about all this southern hospitality, but so far, since we hit Savannah and turned west, everybody treats us like phlegm cups. It was Frankie's idea to take the southerly route to Taos. If it was me, I would have gone to North Dakota and taken a left. See some of those towns where everybody says grace, then eats meat loaf together at big tables and talks about the weather. But Frankie'd never been south of Brockton and it's his car, mine being tied up by the Albright cops due to a vehicular misunderstanding.

"Three bucks." the bartender says, eyeing us like we're curdled milk. It must be a look I inspire because I saw it not a week ago on my ex-wife, Donna, when I told her the band I was in was breaking up and Frankie and I were headed west.

She says to me, "What, you're giving up show bizness?" She can be a real smartass, that one, but then I have my moments, too. I think that might have been what attracted us to each other at first, our mutual ability to insult. That and the fact that in those days we were both sucking up coke like a Hoover demo at Sears. But Donna thought I was hot enough stuff five years ago to marry me. I was up there on stage in my tight big-wad leather pants, faking tough riffs with these stone fingers of mine on a bass guitar. My hair was long and sheeny, too, because all I did was pump gas at the Texaco on Hancock Street and tend bar a couple shifts over at the Dugout. Nobody cared how I looked long as I filled 'em up in either place.

Frankie grabs the Budweiser and chugs it, his Adam's apple skipping up and down his long neck like there's a frog trapped in there. A couple of the local horse rustlers have been watching us and chuckle real loud, like they just remembered some hilarious farmer's daughter joke.

There's a small dance floor and a few good ole boys are sprawled on their dates, swaying to that mournful junk on the jukebox. I notice a few good looking women out there, and one reminds me of Donna the way she fills out her back pockets. Then Frankie starts waving at the bartender like he's ground crew at Logan Airport. I think the guy's ignoring him on purpose, so I start waving, too, because I'm as empty as Frankie and just as thirsty. Driving through the South makes you that way. The bartender finally decides to see what we want and ambles over to us like it's re-cracking his ass to do so. He must have won some award for the highest jeans in town, too.

"What you boys want, wavin' over here like I'm some nearsighted cow?"

"Couple more beers, hey," Frankie tells him.

We get two more Buds slammed down on the dark wood and they both run over.

"This place ain't friendly, Bobby," Frankie says to me. "You think?"

I'm looking at Miss Goodjeans twitching and swaying back from the dance floor. The cowpoke she was dancing with evidently went back to count the stains on his boots and get his buddies to help with the high numbers. I get in her way in a hurry.

"Hi," I say.

"Hey," she says, then pulls a small wad of goo out of her eye. I don't care about this because she's damn good looking and even the Queen of Sheba has a little eye snot and other hygiene puzzles now and then. I'm already thinking Southern.

"Like a drink?"

She gives me a funny look, but I figure it's because she can see better out of the clean eye.

"What kinda drink, honey?" she drawls.

Her calling me honey reminds me of what finally happened with my ex, Donna. A couple years into our marriage, she got a job in one of those heartless insurance agencies out on Route 9, making twice as much as me. Then, after a couple months, she started getting home seven, sometimes eight at night. Now my question was, what happened to that free spirit I did so much blow with who's now selling fucking insurance, and more important, who's buying it that late at night?

I knew Donna was screwing around. I didn't find a love note or nothing, but she told me in a roundabout way. One night she got home about eight and I knew she had a few drinks in her. I'd just been shut out on Final Jeopardy and was feeling sorry for myself that I skipped so much school. I asked her if she wanted to go over to Vinny's Pizza and she said, "Sure, honey, whatever you want to do." Honey. That's what gave it away. I knew then some suit was nailing her 'cuz Donna's not the honey-calling type.

"Whatever you want to drink, I'm you're boy," I tell the cowgirl in front of me. She looks good enough to keep the lights on. We saunter over to the bar together and she gets Mr. Grumpy to serve us up a couple of salty-lipped Margaritas. He's staring at me real hard like I'm standing there with his daughter or something, then takes six bucks out of my ten and spins the change back at me.

Frankie shows up next to us with a woman who looks like Lurch. He loves ugly women, Frankie does, and I think he does it just to be edgy because besides the big strawberry growth on his forehead that looks like an extra asshole, he ain't that bad looking for a drummer.

"Hey, Bobby, this here's Sue Rita. They all got these— whaddya call—double names down here. You notice that?

Sue Rita, Sally Jo, Brenda Lou. What's your name, dahlin'?" Frankie asks my new friend. He's trying to drawl his words, but sounds about as southern as Jack Kennedy.

"Wanda."

"Just Wanda?"

"It's enough, believe me," she says, and we believe her.

I take Wanda back out onto the floor and we slow hunch to some tune that sounds like Tex Ritter trying to climb out of a coma, but I don't care because Wanda's humming along and giving me some ear tongue. What with the beers I had in the car, the ones we could wrestle from the buckaroo behind the bar and Wanda stabbing my ear, I'm revving up pretty good and looking for love in all her wrong places.

When Donna and me broke up, of course I was the one who had to find new digs. Forget her parents had this big house with umpteen rooms where Donna could have hung out for a while. Forget that, I was the one who had to go. When we split, I think it was one of the happiest moments in the lives of Donna's parents. I know our wedding day wasn't. I'm pretty sure they thought I was just another bad phase in their daughter's life. They treated me with a quinella of pity and scorn like you would some guy in a wheel chair who just tipped himself over trying to steal your beer.

Donna made a big deal out of showy dating as soon as I moved out, too. Albright's a big enough town where you could hide that stuff if you wanted to—maybe go to Framingham or even into Boston—but I knew she wanted me to see her with other guys and then go home and think about it. So she'd take to hanging out places where our band played, and then she'd get out there shaking it up on the dance floor while I'm fumbling through riffs I stole from Santana's bass player. I gotta say, that part didn't bother me as much as seeing her go to all that effort at making me feel bad. I think I liked her better when she was just cheating on me and I had to wonder what got her from being nice and cuddly warm to being such a dragon. Could I have caused all that?

I'm getting it on pretty good out here with Wanda, but must have pressed up against the wrong button because she tells me to slow down, she doesn't want to get pregnant in front of the juke box.

"You don't want to ruin those nice, whaddya call 'em, chey-no's, do ya?" she says, blinking at me.

"They ain't chino's," I say, defensively.

"Whatever, it looks like y'all have a roll of quarters in there for Wanda."

I guess it could have been worse: she could have said three bucks worth of dimes. I tell Wanda that I think Frankie needs some companionship because he's got a couple of cowpokes talking to him, but she grabs my arm and gets all snuggly again.

"He can fight his own battles," she says, and it sounds like she knows something about it.

"Well, you know what they say—mi casa, su casa—my battles are your battles," I tell her. From the look on her face, I don't think she did any better in Spanish than I did. I leave her standing there looking like she's ready to procreate and go over to Frankie because Wanda's just a girl in a bar, but Frankie's my drummer.

"Hey, wha's up?" I say to everyone.

One of them—naturally, my luck, the bigger one—stares at me and then suggests a trick of the anatomy involving a pool cue and some kind of automotive lubricant. I can't be sure because he's stupid and he mumbles.

Our band was called "The Magnificent Seven" even though there were only five of us. Most of the time, nobody complained about the count because what we lacked in numbers we made up for in effort. We did a hell of a lot of bouncing around on stage, primarily because between the speed and the coke we all did, everything seemed to be happening in squirrel's time. Bareass on a bareass limb, but it was exciting.

The great thing about the band was we did all covers, no original tunes at all. It didn't start out that way, but the few songs I wrote with our keyboard guy, a future Buddhist named Spike, all sounded like cheap knock-offs. Which they were. If me and Spike put our musical heads together, we wouldn't have made a half-note. So we stuck to covers and focused on hitting the right notes and acting as rock and roll as possible up there on stage.

We became good enough to work the bar circuit up and down Route 9, but to us it felt like we were on tour. We knew we weren't headed for musical history, but the end came suddenly when two of the guys had kids with their girlfriends and sealed their fate when it came to last call. If nothing else, we were a last call band. It seemed to lack the proper glory for a breakup of "The Magnificent Seven," but I'm starting to think glory only exists in the movies.

Frankie's not all that big, two or three inches shorter than I am, which is just below six feet with thick sneakers. But he's a maniac when he gets going—I know because I fought him once. Drinking friends seem to have to do that at least once.

The two high-ass dudes on Frankie's case start turning their bad feelings toward me. "Stay away from Wanda Jean," one of them says.

"Hey, Frankie, she lied to me, she does have two names," I say.

"I think he was tellin' ya to stay out of Wanda's jeans," Frankie says back to me, but looking right at Cowboy Number One.

"You sumnabitches think you can come down here and start rutting our women?" the other guy says.

Rutting's a good word. Maybe it's the tension and all, I don't know, but I laugh out loud when he says this.

"Lemme axe you a question," Frankie says, and just the way he's starting in, I know we're moments away from something real bad. "You boys find it breaks the spell when you're havin' a love moment with your horse and you gotta walk clear around front to get some tongue?"

I called Donna a couple of weeks after she threw me out. It was early on a Tuesday, around seven in the morning. Outside was a low slow sky, the clouds seemed to be pressing down on everything, coating it with a cold iron mist, making it hard to move around without rusting. It was pretty tough looking out a second story room that, for forty bucks a week, provided a view of the train tracks and a shitload of litter. I was on the second floor of the Revere Hotel, just up high enough to break my ankles if I jumped out the window, but too low to kill myself.

"Hullo." A husky voice answered the phone. Some guy. Some fucking guy. Jesus.

"Hello," I said back.

There was an awful pause then and I could hear some rustling.

"Who's this? Kind of early, ain't it?" Then he hung up and left me with the phone humming in my ear, sounding like the warning buzzer for eternity. I don't wish Donna any more trouble in her life, but sometimes I feel like we lost our family before we had a chance to have one.

I don't wait for Frankie's comment to sink in and throw a good short right into the face of the big guy nearest me who goes down like I hit him with a sock full of rocks. I liked that a lot. Frankie misses with a left on his guy but rushes forward to perform his specialty, inside testicle work. We're winning the first five seconds of this round, but I'm not happy to see the big guy bounce up like he has springs in his ass and I'm even less thrilled to see the wave of cowboy hats bobbing toward us. Frankie sees them too and realizes we've started this mess with the door on the other side of the room. We look at each other a second before the crowd arrives and both grin because we've run out of things to do.

"This is going to make us late for Taos," Frankie yells to me.

The first punch takes me high off the forehead and to show how crazy the mind is, I think of a TV show I saw once where this pack of wolves surrounds a wounded elk. The elk doesn't try to get away as the circle tightens around him. He just stands there quietly accepting his fate. And the wolves seem to respect that and finish the job quickly and neatly. But from the look in their eyes, I think most of these boys were tuned in to Hee-Haw that night. I throw a couple harmless jabs into the crowd just to keep my hands busy, but soon the pain of a dozen punches settles in and I brace myself, waiting for the dark needles to take over and hope that these clowns have the sense to know when to stop.

Even before we broke up, I often wondered if Donna was the female version of me and that's what pissed her off so much. We were always pretty good at taking action, but not so good at talking to each other. Isn't that what you're supposed to do nowadays? Communicate?

Just before I go under, for a split second, I can see Donna standing there like the first day I met her. She was tall and slim in tight clothes with a wide smile cranked up just for me. It was before we had a chance to disappoint each other, back when everything was spanking new and our words meant something to each other, something like the first whisper of spring.

The Albright Kid

"I do honor the very flea of his dog."
—Ben Jonson

EVERY TIME Coach Moody hit a sharp ground ball our way, you could see bugs flying out of the grass, and it didn't take much of a genius to figure out these were the first grounders for the bugs this season. It was my turn and with another crack of the bat, a growing white blur snaked and hopped toward me. I charged it wildly, without hope, and felt the ball sting me solidly on the left leg and sit me down. Then I endured the obligatory howls of laughter from the older guys, the 13 and 14 year olds.

"It's OK," I said to them, "I'm a catcher and pitchers don't throw grounders."

I was already making excuses early in life in a small town in Massachusetts on a wicked hot July afternoon in 1959.

We were all dressed the same: blue T-shirts with the camp emblem and blue shorts and sneakers. A lot of knobby knees and big-time dreams and everyone was rammy because the man himself was going to show up. The Kid. It started as one of those crêpe paper fire rumors until Coach Moody, our version of the real truth, gave it the official nod. He would be there that afternoon.

I took my place at the back of the ground ball line and traced the words on Ratty Nelson's shirt with my eyes. Red on blue, the figure swinging the bat stood out like a gladiator, and surrounding it like a halo were the words "Ted Williams Baseball Camp."

By 1959, Eisenhower had given us almost six and a half years of golf and grandfatherly smiles, but kids needed a little more activity out of their heroes. And there were plenty of those giants to go around then too.

The first time I saw Ted Williams in Fenway Park, the number 9 seemed to smile on his back, glad to be there, in crisp afternoon red on that impossibly white uniform. He had all sorts of people hanging around him—sportswriters, ballplayers, cops, ushers, and kids. The kids were the main thing, though. They'd spill out over the railing next to the Red Sox dugout before the game just to stand on the same ground as Ted. The ushers would haul them back into the stands and two minutes later, they'd be back again, as relentless as the tides.

Like every kid, I knew his batting average every time he came up to the plate. It was to be my only painless encounter with math. I knew all his records and stats. I even knew a little of the shaded areas of his life that seeped out of the tight security he held over them, like his divorce and a few public drinking mistakes. But more than anything, I knew his moves.

He had a singular stride to the plate, like a man going to collect an approved loan. Ted took his practice swings a few feet from the batter's box and the catcher always seemed to cringe. And then he would bang the dirt out of his cleats with the bat. He really used to wail away at his cleats. One time in a little league game, I was pounding away at afternoon dust on my rubber cleats, aping Ted, and I missed my shoe, giving my ankle bone a base hit. I had to be helped away from the batter's box by those not too immobile from laughter.

Ted would dig in and wring the end of the bat as he pumped it toward the pitcher. Once, twice. The 9 rode on his back with him in the sun, and his neck would crease as he held his body straight to the plate and look at the pitcher, daring him to throw the ball.

Then came the final wringing of the hands and those slashing, screaming balls he would hit. Sometimes you knew they were gone by the sound of the ball hitting the bat, a sudden sharp violence, and it would turn the hot afternoon around in the stands and bring us to our feet as filled with juice as though we had hit it ourselves.

Coach Moody was through with us. Everyone had his mind on Ted showing up after lunch, and routine grounders were eating up even the good fielders.

"Forget it," Moody finally said, "it's hot, you're not."

We all liked Moody because he really didn't give a damn one way or another, as long as you gave the effort. He had played a couple of seasons with the Tigers a while back and had more than one girlfriend which was sufficient history to win us over right there.

We were on our way to the mess hall for the afternoon swill when another counselor, an ogre named Duffy, caught up to me. Duffy was a frustrated ex-minor leaguer, which may tell you everything there is to know about him, except he didn't really seem to like kids and, I suspected, hated baseball because he never made the big show. He was feared at camp because even dumb kids can sense rancor. Out of all the kids he had his daggers into in 1959, though, no one set him off more than I did.

"Solid work out there on the grounders, Gagger," he sneered at me. Anyone who made an error was a gagger to him.

"I was distracted by the bugs," I told him.

He was about a foot taller than I was and enjoyed every inch. It usually attracted crowds of three or four whenever Duffy started in on me, but on the day Ted was going to show up, the most this little skirmish could muster was one, a ten year old named Jaret Tuttle who didn't like other kids, either.

He was a fat kid who wore a fake gold watch and everyone called him Phlegm. I don't suppose it was easy being called that, but he never made it easy either. The happiest moments he spent in camp were listening to the blasts from Duffy when they were aimed at someone else.

"You think you're hot stuff, huh?" Duffy was almost hissing at me, so I lied.

"No," I said.

Phlegm was jiggling with delight, and while no camp counselor dared slap a kid, the prospect of it always hung over us.

"I stop stuff OK," I reminded Duffy as he began to strut away from me, "I can catch a baseball."

I was never more than average, but still took my baseball pretty seriously and didn't like any other inference, true or otherwise. Duffy took two strides forward and brought his face within an inch of mine until I could smell the blanket of cigarettes on his breath. Phlegm was close to expiring with ecstasy. You wouldn't think a simple remark about being able to catch a baseball could push a guy to the edge, but there Duffy was, certainly teetering. He could barely moves his lips from all the grinding that was going on inside.

"I'll see you in my cabin tonight, asshole," he said and walked quickly away to set up the stretching machine. "Asshole" was about as far as the counselors went in character assassination. Granted, our parents wouldn't have been pleased with it, but we were always impressed whenever anyone got that far along in counselor ire.

"You're going to get it," Phlegm said to me, then looked at that dumb watch and waddled away.

The mess hall was buzzing when we got there and the entire camp had shifted into Ted Williams alert. The usual slurp and gobble at the hall was replaced by a kind of low drone, and the tinkling of glass and silverware sounded like spilled coins.

Phlegm and I were last in line and rewarded with fruit cup and Spaghetti-O's. We sat at our twelve year olds' table and Phlegm started in, telling everyone how Duffy got me again and how I was going to pay big this time for being such an asshole.

106

Like I said, nobody really cared much for Phlegm but everyone liked it a lot when you got into trouble, so they all listened with dopey smiles. I even listened for a while, then I just watched him. Phlegm's eyes squinted and his nostrils flared. He was enjoying this way too much.

I looked down at my lunch and chose a large ripe blueberry and leaned over to Phlegm who was in mid-gesture. I rammed that little purple marble right up his left nostril where it lodged like the ball of a roll-on deodorant bottle. Phlegm was struck dumb, but the rest of the table was thrilled. This was innovation they could admire.

He tried to pick it out but only succeeded in shoving it a little further out of sight. That's when the suggestions began floating around.

"Hawk it out, Phlegm," one kid said.

"Nah, blow it outta there," another yelled, moving his Spaghetti-O's out of the way.

"Squeeze it and sniff," some kid from another table offered.

Phlegm wasn't doing well. He was still in a small state of shock since insertion, and the solutions being fired around the table only overwhelmed him. This must have been his first nose blueberry.

The commotion level rose over all this and sure enough, here came Duffy with a psychotic look on his face.

"Your handiwork?" he fumed, as if he cared about Phlegm.

He made a few more guttural sounds and then, realizing he would be held accountable for any truly heinous public acts, decided to save himself for the evening retribution. For more immediate punishment, Duffy sent me down to the lake to chain the canoes together. Without my Spaghetti-O's, too, which Phlegm had designs on even with a blueberry up his schnoz.

Duffy was a maestro of mental torture and knew what he

was doing by sending me down to the lake. I would miss Ted's arrival. I'd still get to see him, but the project he gave me would take about an hour and Ted was due before that. Every kid in camp would see him before me, have a chance to talk to him. By the time I would see him, he'd be all kidded out.

The walk to the lake was the best part of the camp. Pine trees hung over the trail to form compact and silent green tunnels and prairie warblers darted in and out like yellow rain. Duffy had spun a few gruesome axe murder stories about the lake and ruined the walk for all of us at night, but during daylight hours it was all dappled shadows and pine needles, evergreens and oak. Not much to get spooked over.

The lake was clear and cold and opened up in a crow of nature after the heavily wooded trail. The canoes were strewn haphazardly along the twisting hilly shoreline. I had to grab one, drag it over to the boat shed, walk back and grab another, and stack them three high. Then I had to loop a chain around them so the axe murderers couldn't take them out at night.

It was like all the menial and meaningless jobs adults love to heap on kids as a power move, and it was an agony of fifty minutes before I was through. I was sure Ted had arrived by then and I hurriedly began the trek back. I took the bends in the trail like a tight sports car and then, at the darkest bend of the trail, I ran smack into him.

He was taking the trail to the lake in the opposite direction and there we were. Me and Ted. Ted and me. I could imagine someone saying, "Say, where's Ted?" and the answer would have to be, "Oh, you know, he's over there, with that kid from Albright." Ted and the Albright Kid.

I would have been less startled to run into the Easter Bunny on that path. We stood looking at each other for an instant and I had to crane my neck to look up at him. He seemed a foot taller than even Duffy.

"Hey, kid," he said to me.

"Hi, Ted," I said.

He fidgeted with a key chain. "I always come in the back way so I can come down to the lake first. Always liked this walk. You going back up to camp?"

I nodded idiotically, as though I could fit that into my schedule.

"Well, c'mon," he said turning and brushing me lightly, "we'll walk back together. I can always see the lake another time."

He kept a hand on my shoulder as if to steer me on the trail. I wished my Dad could have seen that one. As we cleared the trail and sauntered past the mess hall toward the flagpole, we left a cluster of mouths agape and grimy pointing fingers marked our way. Me and Ted. Back from our casual walk, fresh from one-on-one talk.

Ted started waving to the other kids, so I did, too, like the President's wife from the back of a car. Out of the corner of my eye, I saw Duffy slinking off toward his cabin and I gave him the biggest big wave.

That afternoon, standing sixty feet from the pitching machine, Ted hit us fly balls so high the blue took over the ball and made it disappear for an instant. I never caught one. I just kept looking at him, the most perfect thing I had seen in my young life, frozen in time in that batting cage.

He dug into the dirt with his cleats and wrung the end of the bat dry. The force of his presence almost seemed to disturb the air around him, as if his power to be there, at that time and in that spot, was mandated by his great will which gave no regard to the earthly summons of space and gravity.

The mechanical arm of the machine paused momentarily at the top of its arc and then came down, whipping a fast ball in on him. With a wring of his hands and a casual flick of his wrists, The Kid carried the ball far out into the day. I knew then, standing there in the outfield, that something special had happened to me, something I could always re-visit but never give back.

Later that evening I would face Duffy's wrath, but if nothing else, those towering fly balls gave me a sense of myself, too. I understood for the first time that all this would pass, that all things do, and that our lives are comprised of these moments, lucky and otherwise. Even as it was happening, I knew I'd remember this particular day for the rest of my life, a day charged with charm, where I stood under a fly ball and wondered if it would ever come down to earth.

Another Wonder of the World

"A friend may well be reckoned the masterpiece of Nature."
—Ralph Waldo Emerson

YOU WOULD have figured Tony D'Allesandro would be plenty pissed at having his nose whacked off, but when I tried to ask him about it he just moaned through his bloody handkerchief. It must have hurt like hell because Tony's as tough as they come. We were careening our way to Albright Hospital, hanging on for dear life because Fogarty was behind the wheel, aiming that '79 Chrysler boat of his at a rate of speed that made losing a nose seem like a viable option.

"Jesus Christ," Fogarty kept saying, like a mantra. "Jesus Christ."

"We're going to meet old Jesus if you don't slow this heap down," I yelled from the back seat. "Take it easy. Tony's going to live."

I wasn't real sure of that. D'Allesandro tried to speak, but it drifted out the hole in his face and sounded bubbly, making Fogarty gag. Tony was never what you would call a great looking guy anyway, but without his nose he was going to be uglier than Ethel Merman's autopsy.

"Tony, it don't look bad, man," I said, pressing my hand on his shoulder. "Honest. It might hurt like hell, but it don't look bad."

"Dabb uuuer haaw ooof ha uu-in shuuwer," Tony said, which I had an inkling meant, "Take your hand off my fucking shoulder!"

We blew past a school bus so fast none of the kids had the chance to give us the finger. A few minutes later, we skidded to the emergency room entrance in a hail of dirt and grit that sent a few surgeons scurrying from their cigarette break.

Fogarty's Chrysler shuddered like a stallion and Tony jumped out to head into the hospital. I thought he had a head of steam up, but then he started to teeter. He did a half pirouette—damned if it wasn't almost graceful—but then ruined the number by throwing up. In terms of nastiness, a guy with no nose throwing up was about the worst thing I'd seen and judging from these guys in the green pajamas who scattered as though we had just lobbed a grenade, it seemed to rank high on their lists as well.

A couple of beefy guys finally came out and threw Tony on a rolling stretcher, pushing him inside, where a nurse the size of Fogarty's Chrysler blocked us from going into the emergency room. She looked down at Tony and paled. "Family only, take a seat. Could we get him cleaned up, please?"

Then we're all standing around waiting for the lowest person on the medical ladder to show up and hose old Tony down for the doctor. Me and Fogarty were hustled into a waiting room filled with Kiwanis Magazines and worried people. Some character with long sideburns paced back and forth, muttering under his breath. He was in a softball uniform with the name *Henry's Erections* emblazoned on the chest in purple and gold.

"Never hit a line drive like that in my life," he said aloud to anyone in the room who gave a shit. "And he stops it with his head."

Fogarty leaned over to me and said quietly, "You think Tony's going to have to wear one of those silver noses like Lee Marvin in "Cat Ballou?"

I met Fogarty and D'Allesandro in the fifth grade when they bummed a couple of cigarettes off me at recess. We've been off and on together ever since high school. We worked for the town together, then we went in the Army together on the buddy plan, but they immediately sent us to different parts of the United States. Just missed Vietnam. Then we wound up back working for the town again. We suffered the Red Sox tragedies together, our divorces (Tony is in the lead with two), and the awkwardness we feel around our kids even though they're all adults. We're back working for the town again and now that we're forty-eight, we've pretty much become our fathers.

They were good pals themselves and used to take us on camping trips up to the White Mountains before we were teenagers. We loved those trips because our fathers let us get roaring shitfaced with them. That didn't last long because Fogarty's mom smelled a rat when her son came home after one of our father-son trips and spent the rest of the day gacking into the toilet.

"Altitude fever," Mr. Fogarty tried to explained.

There's some people in Albright who might think our dads were a trio of fuckups, but I got nothing but good to say about all three of them. We loved each other the best way we could, and they're all dead now, so what's it matter? Tony said one time that we act like our dads because that's the only way to keep them alive, which would make him the world's greatest noseless philosopher.

This whole mess with Tony started one night about a month ago when Fogarty and I were in the Frontier, a gin mill under the Revere Hotel that shook every time a train went by twenty yards away. We were hunched over on our bar stools, airing out our cracks and lying to each other, when Tony walked in and said, "Gentlemen, tonight we enter the arena of entrepreneurs."

Fogarty and I looked at him and, out of courtesy, didn't roll our eyes. Most of the time he says that it either costs us money, embarrassment, or the threat of 90 days.

"Hey Tony, no offense," Fogarty said, "But I'm still paying off the credit card on those coolie hats from Saigon. You know, the ones you said every gardener from Framingham to Falmouth would want."

"Ho Chi Minh City," Tony corrected. "And I was supposed to know they'd all be size six?"

We've had this conversation before, so it's almost like being in a play. Our last venture, selling shrimp out of the back of Tony's pickup, could have been okay, but once someone cracked the first frosty of the day, we started in on the shrimp and when Fogarty came back from 7-11 with cocktail sauce, we were doomed. We ate so many shrimp that our iodine counts shot through the stratosphere. A guy Fogarty knew gave me a grapefruit injection that seemed to help.

Tony rolled up his sleeves. "Boys, everything else has been a warm-up for this. All practice. Because now we're going into a business that is the backbone of our country. Where is more goddamned land wasted than on the golf courses of America? We're going to slice into that pie."

Fogarty and I looked at him as if he were a minor Disney character. He expected as much and smugly crossed his arms, waiting.

I went first. "Hey, Tony, great idea. We'll just go buy up a couple hundred acres of prime land. Maybe put a small pond on it, too. I hear you can get a lot of extra golf balls that way."

Fogarty quit playing with the Heineken coaster—the closest he'd ever get to a beer that good—and said, "I hate fucking golf. I hate golfers and I hate that dumb-shit polite applause the crowd makes on TV. Sounds like they're all wearing gloves. And I really hate when some jagoff announcer calls a putt courageous. Davey Crockett's courageous, not some asshole in cranberry pants."

Tony nodded his head up and down. I would have felt a sense of *déjà vu*, except there was no *déjà* about it. We'd been down these roads before. One of the reasons Tony is more the leadership type is that he can read minds.

"I know you guys have heard this shit before," he said to us, motioning to the bartender, Henry Vaughan, for another round. We waited for Henry to make his long, slow trek down the bar. At an age when most guys were trying to remember their kids' names, Vaughan still put in an eight hour shift, serving shots, beer, and pretzels to executive customers like us.

"We're not going to open up a regular golf course, for Christ's sake. That takes Trump money. But you know that mess over in North Albright, that thing they were hoping would catch on as an industrial park? Well, the rent's cheaper than Betty Falconi and I've got a site picked out."

Tony paused to allow for any late entry sarcasm and then, probably because he was getting to the good part, clammed up as Henry approached with the refills.

"We're not going to open up some huge place, boys," he said, watching Henry walk away for the fifteen minute trip down to the other end of the bar. "We're going into the big, little time—miniature golf."

I looked at Fogarty who was looking at me and both of us seemed to be wondering if this was a good thing. It was sure nothing I ever thought of, but then that would include lots of ideas. Tony draped his heavy arms over us.

"I'm not talking some half-ass deal here, guys. None of that bogus windmill and happy whale shit, either," Tony said. "We're going to open the world's first X-rated miniature golf course."

Oh, well, that's different.

The next morning we met at the Albright Industrial Park, a failed attempt to attract businesses into depressed North Albright, and now little more than a forlorn gravel pit with a few aluminum buildings. There were currently only two businesses located there—Home Away From Home, storage sheds for pack rats who couldn't bring themselves to throw shit away and an equipment rental company called Richard's Rentals that everyone in town called Dick's Big Equipment. We considered that a good omen.

Tony's concept was pretty simple. Instead of the standard obstacles like a happy-looking lighthouse where you putt the ball into the front door and it trickles out the back, we would substitute a body orifice. Since it was to be a nine hole course and we didn't want to repeat a hole, we needed to use both sexes. Tony explained that this gave us the added bonus of eliminating any potential sexual discrimination charges, thereby appearing modern and enlightened.

The first thing we had to do was level off the land, and when that nearly killed us after an hour, we hired one kid from the storage sheds and another from Dick's Big Equipment to help us. They were thrilled because they were getting paid by us and their employers at the same time, a lesson in double dipping that would help them later if they went into politics.

Soon enough we were ready for the design phase, and here's where it got a little tricky. We all showed up at the Albright Miracle Diner out on Route 9 that night to establish the layout of the course and have some of the meatloaf special. Unfortunately, the only thing Fogarty or I could draw were flies and while D'Allesandro was no Degas, at least his drawings were recognizable.

So Tony was in the middle of drawing his concept of the golf putter, which was nothing more than a long skinny pecker with a flat head, when the 70 year old waitress, Rhonda, came by to unload the meatloaf. She took one look at the drawing on the placemat, two looks at us, and started hollering for the owner, a retired wrestler who grappled under the name of Deadbolt, the Apostle of Mayhem. You could sense immediately that dessert would be out of the question.

We ran into a guy at the Frontier two nights later named Moe Greenblatt and he told us that he used to be a caricature artist in Provincetown and had drawn everything humanly imaginable, including a few things that would never have occurred to him.

Tony explained his concept to Moe. "We want to walk that fine line between good taste and downright nasty."

"Tony, for Christ's sake," Fogarty said. "how can a putter that's a big schlong and a basket of hairy golf balls be in good taste?"

D'Allesandro narrowed his eyes and looked from me to Fogarty to our new design consultant who was slumping down toward the table, a victim of his drink limit for the second time that day. "Don't let him go into that beer puddle, he'll drown," Tony said. "Listen, either one of you ever heard of the Colossus of Rhodes?"

"Somethin' to do with the Big Dig?" I said, mostly kidding. Fogarty snorted.

"The Colossus of Rhodes is one of the eight wonders of the world and we have a chance to create another one right here. People are going to flock to North Albright because we have something no one else in the world has. Think of the photos alone for the customers. Can't you just see Grampa waving his putter around like the old days? Guys, it might be Albright this year, but tell me you don't catch a whiff of that thing called 'franchise?' We could be sitting on another wonder of the world. This might be the Big Mac of golf sex."

Say what you will about D'Allesandro, but there were times when he was goddamned Knute Rockne to me. I was four beers inspired and ready that minute to cut out plywood buttocks, sand down gigantic breasts, and make sure the nuts on the seventh hole were plumb to the green.

When we met Moe at the Frontier the next morning, we had to reintroduce ourselves, but after a couple of breakfast drafts and a few hasty drawings, we knew we had the right guy. It turned out that Moe Greenblatt could flat out draw body parts—he was the Goya of Gonads.

We went to work. A great deal of our material came from what we could scrounge or, more often, steal from the town. I worked on one of the highway department trucks, so I could always grab a half sheet of plywood here and there. D'Allesandro worked at the dump, so he was always fighting with the dump pickers over the best stuff. Fogarty usually mowed the three cemeteries in town and was left alone for the most part. He was a reliable source for flowers.

The work in North Albright began in earnest. Since I shook less than Fogarty, I was the jigsaw man, carving hams and flanks out of quarter inch plywood. Then Tony put Fogarty's shakes to good use by giving him sandpaper. Moe went to work next, some days barely able to stand, but always engrossed in whatever piece of plywood anatomy he was handed. He was one of the great X-rated miniature golf artists of his time.

And Tony was in his element, too, supervising everything and enforcing quality control. One night Moe had to be cut back on his beer ration after he drew a Groucho face on a nipple, but nothing more serious than that.

Incredibly, in less than a week, even with our financing the way it was, everything was as close as we were going to get. I'll be damned if it didn't look as good as any other horseshit miniature golf course you see at the side of the road.

Tony decided we should name the place, *Romance Golf*, which we all thought was to the point. But we hadn't budgeted anything for publicity, so Moe offered to paint *Romance Golf* on his back and walk through downtown Albright until he was arrested. I was most impressed with the magnitude of the offer and wanted to make Moe a full partner, but we never got the chance for a board of director's meeting because Albright's Building Inspector, Arnold

Sadowski, showed up as unannounced as Pearl Harbor.

Sadowski was a former Albright High classmate, one of those kids in school who never fit into a nickname. Ski was far too manly and what are you going to do with the name Arnold? We would have called him Rat, for always squealing on his classmates, except Debby Girard already had that name thanks to her rodent-like features and admitted passion for cheese. Now we had to endure the hulking adult Sadowski, the product of all our former taunting and cruelty, but far worse, a guy with local power and a memory for grudges. You'd have to get in line to hate this slug and he'd grown to love the power of that.

"Well, well, well," he said, like he was a Texas Ranger instead of building inspector. "Which one of you geniuses is in charge of this enterprise?" Then he looked over at me as though something unspeakable perched on my shoulder. "And why am I not surprised," he said, pointing his finger at me, "that where Fogarty and D'Allesandro are, you're right there with them, up to your neck."

"Well you know us, Arnold," I said, cheerfully, "three amigos."

"Sure. Where's D'Allesandro? I need to talk to someone smarter than my lunch."

"He's out adjusting the hinges on number five's chastity belt," Fogarty said.

I think that made Sadowski really looked around for the first time. "Holy shit," he said. "What the hell kind of perv shit is all this?"

Tony's layout had been masterful, from the very first hole of a harmless cutout of a big pair of lips with a tongue for a ramp, to the final hole, Moe's masterful orgy scene with fourteen different orifice options. Sadowski began scribbling on a pad of paper and then brayed about zoning regulations, building permits, and the Legion of Decency. He might as well have been speaking in tongues for all the attention we were going to give him. Fogarty and I headed for the beer cooler.

Even considering all that, we might have gotten away with things. I was ready to make Sadowski a full time partner, too, just for the building permit, but then he saw that fateful eighth hole and that's what cost D'Allesandro his nose.

It was a par four hole, made difficult by having to putt around a meaty thigh—what golfers might call a dogleg left. When you got around that, you were rewarded with a large rendering of a beautiful heart-shaped ass that had a curious configuration on the left cheek. It was supposed to be a series of blemishes which, if connected like dots, distinctly resembled the profile of Richard Nixon. And it was Tony's dumb luck that he had just drawn the blemishes in and was standing there admiring his work.

Sadowski looked at him, then looked at the big plywood ass and suddenly went bonkers, running for his car and hollering. Fogarty and I looked at each other baffled, but when Sadowski came back waving a claw hammer in the air like Magua, we took cover behind Dick's Big Equipment.

Sadowski headed for D'Allesandro who was now behind the plywood ass, tightening something or other. When he stood up and saw Sadowski in his face, he looked pretty surprised, but when Sadowski took a swipe at him and caught Tony on the nose with the claw, he looked real surprised.

This was followed by a pretty hefty yell which I'd guess was Tony saying goodbye to his nose. And while neither Fogarty or I could be janitors at a mensa meeting, it didn't take a genius to figure out that Sadowski's wife was the inspiration for those dots and Tony D'Allesandro had been connecting them for the past few months when Sadowski wasn't home. That's what we learned later, anyway.

Of all the wives in Albright Tony's got to get down and bony with, he picks Myra Sadowski. That's just the kind of bad luck that dogs drinking men to their graves.

I called the cops right away and Moe Greenblatt had the pleasure of squealing on Sadowski because we were already long gone on the way to the hospital. No sense in waiting for an ambulance when you have a Chrysler.

As for D'Allesandro, when they finally let us in to see him, he still didn't look too great. I have a hunch he's going to have to work more on his personality to make up for this loss of nose. Hell, I would have given Tony half my nose if Fogarty chipped in part of his, but being Irish, Fogarty didn't have any to spare.

But I'll tell you the kind of guy Tony is. He told us he wasn't going to press charges against Sadowski. He had to repeat it three times because we couldn't understand him, but I thought that was what you'd call a Christian gesture. I heard the next day, when the cops brought Sadowski in to apologize, Tony asked him what he was going to do now that Myra knew what an orgasm was. Tony's quick, even with a piece of his face missing.

It's a funny thing about how people come to think of you in a town where you spend your whole life. And I know a few of them call us the Repeat Boys, because we're a bunch of fuckups like our old men. Well, we might have missed some glory days but we've never lost each other. I think there's some muscle in that—in having people you can count on.

Fogarty said to us one night, "You know, you guys are not only the best friends I've ever had in the world, but the only ones who still talk to me."

And who knows, now that we've got this space in North Albright and the town's a little nervous about Tony suing them, we might put our heads together and come up with another wonder of the world. Don't count us out, America.

Paradise Dance

"I don't think anybody should write his autobiography until after he's dead."—Samuel Goldwyn

THERE WAS a letter from Margaret in my faculty box at Albright High School where I teach English. I knew it was from her by the painful quake of the handwriting on the face of the envelope where my name, *Herbert Pruett*, was scrawled, then the school address carefully etched below that. The only other thing remarkable about this letter was that Margaret had been dead for two months.

"Fan mail?" A voice behind me asked.

That would be Julia Finchner, a ninth grade geography teacher with coffee saucer eyes and an unfortunate quiver to her upper lip as though she had just bitten into something unexpectedly chalky. Julia and I dated briefly when I came to Albright High eight years ago, but it was more a matter of convenience than mutual attraction. We had both been recently divorced, had cleared the over-40 bar, and our classrooms shared a water fountain. It wasn't exactly Casablanca in the panorama of great romances, but we both took what we could get, burning out on each other long before ignition.

"Hey, Julia," I said, ignoring her question.

Julia and I didn't like each other enough to alter the new privacy our divorces offered. And to be fair, Julia's affections also may have been hampered by my fussy nature, conspicuous frugality, and thick aviator-style eyeglasses she once said made me look like a surfacing snorkler.

For my part, I was both fascinated and repelled by her bird-like mannerisms, especially with a name like Finchner.

"Jeez, I didn't know you got your personal mail here,"

Julia said. Her petite salt and pepper head bobbed forward. Peck. Peck. Peck.

"It's cheaper than a post office box," I said cheerfully and headed for the parking lot, greeted by a stiff northeasterly breeze. Whatever Julia had to say next was cut off by the automatic door closing. My Toyota Corolla sat in its faded glory in the faculty section of the parking lot, 275,000 miles of corrosion which, based on their expressions, irritated several of my SUV-commando colleagues. I got into the car and gently placed Margaret's letter on the seat next to me, unopened. I felt a certain sense of propriety towards the envelope, as if it would be offensive to give it a hasty read while fighting traffic.

I was two months from fifty now, and hadn't published anything beyond my phone number in fifteen years. The promising flame from my first collection of stories had long ago extinguished. My ex-wife Alexis theorized I used up all that promise in the first effort. She delivered this encouraging nugget a few minutes after her lawyer picked me apart in front of Judge Patricia Rodriguez—known in Albright barber shops and barrooms as "Pit Bull Patty." But truth should never be a culprit; Alexis was right, my life had been constructed on that one bright moment: thirteen stories about paternal angst by a childless author.

As soon as I got back to my apartment, I poured myself a large Early Times, threw in a couple of ice cubes, and held the envelope up to the light. I imagined hearing Margaret's flat Boston accent call impatiently from inside. It had been an unmistakable voice, low and breathless, and when she used my first name, she ignored the r's, but bolstered the b, so when she said, "Herbert," it came out, "Heah-*But!*"

It wasn't Margaret's diction that brought her into my life, though, it was her music. I had gone out to the Albright Manor Nursing Home to lead a ten-week memoir-writing workshop, the result of an unexpected feel-good-about-ourselves grant from the local arts council.

From the winding driveway, the rest home rose from the tangled drab of abandoned cranberry bogs and a long-forgotten farm. The building sat on the crown of a small hill, one of those long, rambling ranch styles, all one level, and designed in a stroke of architectural horseplay to provide a clear view of the Albright Memorial Cemetery through a stand of bleak locust trees.

The activities director met me at the door, an attractive fortyish woman who buzzed through the difficult consonants of her last name, then extended a hand in greeting.

"Your class is very excited about this, Mr. Pruett," she said. "You'll find them in the rec room, just down the corridor to the right."

I mumbled a suggestion she call me Herb, thanked her, and walked down the long, polished corridor to the rec room, accompanied by someone playing the piano. I knew it was not unusual in a rest home with 56 women and two genetically fortunate men that someone played the piano. What was unusual was the low puff of sound that preceded the notes a moment before they were played. The voice was not always on key and the piano was not that much more precise in locating the melody, but the two entangled in a harmony that sounded as though it came from a mysterious and primitive instrument.

My writing group was seated around a table, chatting away with each other, so I stepped over to the piano to acknowledge Margaret's playing. Her broad back sheltered the piano keys, and she played the same melody over and over, quickening the pace slightly, as if trying to bully her way through a difficult passage. I looked over her shoulder at the hands splayed along the teeth of the keyboard and saw they were severely twisted and crimped.

The index finger on her right hand bent at a nearly right angle and her middle finger contorted in the opposite direction. The rest of her fingers fared no better, yet through this tangle of age and arthritis, a melody surfaced from the piano in a halting collaboration with her voice. And it was uncanny how closely Margaret's voice won the race with the notes, as though on the same tether, but a knot apart.

"Nola."

I turned to look into the face of one of my writing students, a Mrs. Ivy Pritchard, according to her name tag. "That's what Margaret is playing," she said. "It's called 'Nola,' and she plays it quite a bit. You'll see. But we should start the class soon because some of us have Microwave Magic at three-thirty.

I learned quickly that at Albright Manor, time was measured with great respect. I hurried over to the table with a show of enthusiasm, scrubbing my hands together. Then Mrs. Pritchard asked in her small voice, "Before we get started, where exactly do you stand on the Shakespearean question, Mr. Pruett? Are you an Oxfordian, or not?"

They were an interesting and lively group and we started with a discussion of favorite authors. I lead good book discussions because reading is what writers do when they are afraid of writing. That, and watching a lot of action videos which seems to gratify any genetic impulse to exercise. The group, ten in all, regaled each other with their favorites. Many were surprisingly current in their reading—a woman with heavy blue eye shadow *adored* T. Coraghessan Boyle, and another who looked older than Rome but went by the name of Bunny, had just completed her fifth Anne Tyler. There were Updike fans and two Maeve Binchys, and someone named Thelma had been reading "Bridges of Madison County" for the past year and a half, even though half a dozen people had already told her the ending. The lone man in our group, a Mr. Shapiro, reported that he was reading "I, the Jury" and Mel Tormé's biography simultaneously.

The rest of the hour went quickly, more like a gossip session where we maligned hard-working writers whose weekly output of words were in excess of what I'd churned out in the past three years.

"What about these auto-watcha' call 'em we're gonna do," Mrs. D'Aggastino asked, "these memories?"

"Memoirs?" I asked.

"That's it. Memoirs. French stories."

Mrs. Hancock said. "I may have done some foolish things in my life, but I don't want to sound like a fool telling about them."

Mr. Shapiro stood, evidently a dramatic gesture that represented the class's enthusiasm, and hiked his pants up to just below his breasts. "That's where you come in, Herb," he said to me. "You're going to keep us from sounding like fools."

After class the activities director reintroduced herself this time as Cookie. It felt funny to call a grown woman Cookie until I remembered my 78-year-old student, Bunny. But Cookie's last name was something like "Smerzynski" and I'm stumbly enough without trying that out.

I made a fuss over gathering my papers while she approached. She was alluring in a hardy New England way, tall and big boned, the kind of woman you'd be willing to hitchhike with. She carried herself with an earned confidence and managed to be attractive, thanks largely to a crinkly good humor in her eyes and a deep-dimpled smile that displayed a small overbite. Her attractiveness was more a sum of the parts and, though Cookie might have been a lot closer to 50 than 40, she stood out like Lolita in this crowd.

"So how'd the class go, Mr. Pruett?" she asked.

I was disappointed she didn't call me Herb because it obliged me to be formal and make a stab at her last name.

"Oh, it was fine, Ms. Smerzzyzz. . . ." I tried not to spray her.

She smiled, obviously accustomed to surname abuse.

"Why don't you just use Cookie like everyone else?"

"Herb," I answered back, and we shook hands.

Her smile carved two creases at the sides of her mouth, then she lowered her voice and said, "I heard Margaret delayed your class this afternoon. Sometimes she forgets where she is when she's playing the piano."

"She didn't delay anything. I was the one hanging around listening to her. I found her music to be pretty intriguing."

Cooke tilted her head back to laugh and I glanced into her mouth, the overhead fluorescent light winking off her dental work.

"Intriguing it is, Herb."

We started to walk toward the front entrance. Cookie's hair was puffed up on top, not quite a beehive, maybe a lower squirrel's nest. She might have put her ensemble together in the spirit of the place, too, but she could have dressed a lot younger. Definitely go with a wrist watch instead of that ponderous watch that hung around her neck like a large round biscuit, the only convenience being I could check on the time while gawking at her breasts, which were as substantial as the rest of her.

"I liked how personal her playing seemed," I said, noticing it was a little after 4:30.

Cookie smiled professionally. "Perhaps we're more used to her playing," she said. "Margaret hasn't missed a day at that piano since she got here six months ago. Not a day. The same tune, basically."

We reached the door. "Well," I said, checking her time again. That overbite was growing on me, too.

"Yes, well," she said, turning her watch over. "See you next week then, Mr. Pruett."

"I look forward to it, Ms. Smrzzz. . . ."

This is a fair representation of my inability to generate sparks with women. Even my marriage to Alexis, a woman who could pry sparks out of any man—and did out of many—failed to teach me anything about the cryptic society of women.

Her friends couldn't understand why she had chosen me over the horde of men available to her. I couldn't either, but I was so happy about it, I wasn't about to ask. When Alexis and I really began to know each other, by the third month of our marriage, I realized with a sinking heart that I was merely a player in the Alexis Marital Phase. By our eighth month together it was obvious she was rapidly outgrowing the phase. As desperately as I wanted to keep her, I could feel our marriage leaving by the front door—exactly what Alexis did six weeks before our first anniversary. She did have the courtesy to leave a note:

> Dear Herb,
>   No spark.
>   Sorry, Alexis

Never had such a minimalist nailed it with fewer words.

I arrived at Albright Manor early the next week and went straight to the rec room. The ensemble of voice and piano drifted into the corridor and when I presented myself in front of the piano, it was as an unabashed fan. She looked up at me and continued to play. It was the first time I actually studied Margaret's face and saw that time had sculpted it gracefully, despite the ravages of her hands. It was large and chiseled, crosscut with the lines of her many years. Her eyes were pale blue and alert, and she had a high, thin nose and tightly pursed lips.

Margaret continued to meet my gaze, then the tune slowed and began to soften. She played quietly, her lips moving as though divulging a secret. Then, as she exhaled the note in a half breath, the piano rushed to join her.

I leaned in and said, "I know that song is called 'Nola,'

and I like it very much, especially the way you play it, Margaret."

She stopped and placed her hands in her lap and looked at me with a slight smile on her face. Then she kept looking.

"Margaret, you're staring at me," I said, smiling.

She nodded. "It's a privilege afforded the very young and the very old," she said. She glanced down at her hands, then back at me. "You know a lot about me—my name, the song I play—but I don't know you."

She made a short movement with her head then, as though tossing off curls that once lived on her shoulder. It was a peculiarly girlish gesture for such an elderly woman.

"Ms. Smerzz, ah, Cookie told me about you," I said. "I'm Herb Pruett."

"Oh yes, the writing teacher. You're the writing teacher and I'm the piano player. We might have been a team in vaudeville. Do you know where the name Margaret comes from? It's Greek and it means Pearl. When I was a girl, our schoolmaster told us where our names came from and what they meant. Some of my friends were fish or mountains, and some were blackbirds and trees. But I was a pearl and I always loved the thought of that."

"You play like a pearl," I said, and saw by the expression on her face that I had made a fortunate remark. It armed me with enough confidence to continue. "I know our class cuts into your playing time but would you consider joining the workshop? We're writing our memoirs and I'd love to read about Nola."

Margaret stood without speaking, wavering slightly as she straightened to her full height, which was, surprisingly, tall enough to look me directly in the eye. She seemed to tire suddenly, but nodded to me before shambling off, never looking back, all the way out the door and into the hall.

The memoir workshop turned into a pleasant surprise.

Each week they brought in sections they'd been working on and read them aloud, then quietly endured the most benevolent questions from the rest of us. They wrote small episodic highlights of their lives, never more than one or two page sketches, some of them dictated to Cookie who typed them up. And no matter how ordinary the scenario—a first kiss, a lost class ring, a long red dress—it always had that delicious sense of eavesdropping.

There were odd turns of phrases worth stealing, too, such as Mrs. Hastings' synopsis of her husband, "His name was William, but he was not the kind of man you'd call Bill."

Occasionally their words sang off the paper with life. A trip into Worcester as a little girl for Mrs. Phillips rivaled a Lewis and Clark adventure along the Snake River. Mrs. Cranhauer's fender bender on the Boston Post Road in 1948 read like a replay of the Hindenburg. And Mr. Shapiro insisted on using the work "tumescent" three times in his narration, but wrote poignantly about his first love. These were gently rendered tales from polite minds, sometimes tender, and always a bit sad because of time's irreverence.

There were days I'd go home after reading their anecdotes and stare hopelessly at the meager debris of my own work. No sparks there, either, Herb. My stories felt stiff and cumbersome, and invariably I'd turn away from my desk, glumly aware of their silence.

I tried to arrive early each week to spend time with Margaret before class, and I always found her arched over the keyboard with a melody, usually "Nola," struggling to rise from the piano. She would speak to me softly at first, as if gauging the range of her voice. We talked about animals and the beach. We talked about inventors and favorite writing pens. Birthstones and the Boston Braves. I barely kept up my end of the conversation, even when we talked about Herb Pruett.

It wasn't until the fourth week that I stumbled onto a way

to get Margaret to talk about herself. We began by talking about movies, and when silent film stars became the subject, Margaret took over in the excitement of reliving 1924.

"I played piano in the theater for the pictures, you know," she said. "I'd take the trolley down street into Albright Center and walk over to the Paradise Theater. It had been built only a year before and it was a wonderful place with lush velvet curtains and deep soft chairs. And clean? Oh my, there was always the aroma of soap or fresh paint. I'm sure it's all gone now, Herbert."

"Not at all. As a matter of fact, they refurbished the Paradise a few years ago," I said.

"Well, my piano was in the corner to the right of the screen, just off a small stage. I'd have to crane my neck to see what was on the screen, then I'd just play whatever came to mind. 'Nola' always went so well with love stories because it's such a happy melody."

I could hear Mr. Shapiro holding court with the ladies over my shoulder, and took it as a signal to get started.

"That's a lot of influence to have, Margaret," I said. "To add music to film nowadays people get paid thousands of dollars."

"I never thought of it as having influence."

"Margaret, why don't you join us? Wouldn't you like to share all that with everyone?"

I hoped our developing friendship would make a difference, but Margaret waved off the suggestion with a pass of her hand and stood, backing away from the piano. I moved forward, giving her an awkward hug.

"I won't ask again," I said. "I want to be a friend, not a pest."

She patted me on the arm and turned to leave. It wasn't until after I read Mrs. Favorini's recollection of sheep shearing in Hyannis during the depression that I noticed Margaret had taken a chair in the corner of the rec room.

I went to Cookie's office after class, a habit I was cultivating. The door was open, so I walked in without knocking and saw Cookie at her desk with head down and her hands on her forehead. It wasn't until I startled her with a throat clearing that she raised her head and I saw the sadness ringing her eyes.

"Ah. Sorry," I said. "Should have knocked. Tough day?"

She showed me a little more of that overbite in an attempt to smile. "Tough decade," she said, then spit out a chuckle. I'd thought a lot about Cookie since my first day at Albright Manor, but for some reason I never imagined her life beyond this place.

"Would you like to have a cup of coffee and talk about it?" I asked. It sounded so blunt, I nearly winced.

"Not at this hour," Cookie said, rubbing her eyes. "I'd be up all night."

"No, I meant, well, coffee, no, just not being here," I stammered. "You know, going somewhere else and sitting and, well, having a conversation."

She smiled. "Herb, are you asking me out on a date?"

Date. The way she said it—DATE—made my offer sound more like RAPE.

"Well, I didn't mean. . . ."

"I'll take a rain check," she said, sitting up straight. "But let's make it a drink. And while I think of it, your workshop seems to be going over well. Good job. Are you enjoying it?"

I tried to look as nonchalant as possible, but I so thirsted for reassurance in my life that I wound up red-faced and speechless, rocking in my shoes. I nodded agreement to the rain check, the compliment, and anything else she had to offer in one overwrought bob of the head. Then I backed out of Cookie's office.

Around the sixth week of the workshop, I ducked out of Albright High immediately after the bell for a study hall I was monitoring, leaving the students alone to complete their plans for the overthrow of the government through hip hop and vegetarianism. I went straight to Albright Manor, hoping to cram in some more mortifying moments with Cookie. She wasn't in her office, but I heard Margaret's music trickling down the gleaming hallway, so I decided to spend the extra time with her.

Margaret and I were so comfortable with each other now that we could both sit and listen to her music as though someone else were playing it. Today she started to talk to me over the melody, punctuating our conversation with her lyrical grunts. She stopped playing and dropped her hands in her lap.

"Earlier, I'd been thinking about a film I played for," she said. "And the more I thought of it, the more I started to lean over, thinking I had to see the screen to know what to play. Just like I did at the Paradise."

She shook her head slowly and smiled.

"What was the film, Margaret?" I asked, sliding a bit in the naugehyde chair.

"Oh you'd never know it. These games we play where you try to name the movie star? You're not very good at it anyway, Heah—*but*."

"All my knowledge is theoretical," I said, chuckling. "You have a clear advantage having lived through it."

"I can't remember the name of the film anymore, but I can picture Mae Marsh up there on the screen and she looked just as pretty as anyone could. I remember that like yesterday, Heah—*but*. Imagine that, I haven't been inside that theater in over 50 years and I can still smell the clean carpet."

"What did your husband do?" I asked her.

She looked down at the keys of the piano. "Oh, he died, Heah—*but*. That's what he did, he died."

The word *died* seem to go on forever, thumping around our heads and through the room until it was finally replaced by a droning diatribe of Mr. Shapiro.

But I didn't get up right away because after looking at Margaret's face, I regretted my curiosity. This keyless entry into the lives of our memoir writers made me expect the same accessibility from Margaret. I was about to apologize when Mr. Shapiro walked over to us and quietly said to me, "Wrote something about my honeymoon in New Hampshire fifty-five years ago. You might want to give it the once over first. It's fairly carnal."

I nodded and got up, reaching out for Margaret's hand as I did so. She took it lightly, allowing me to lead her to a chair within eavesdropping range of the group. And then, as I walked over to the table of ten eager memoirists, I had an idea that seemed so right I could scarcely contain myself during Mrs. Willett's rendering of the first time she flew in a DC-3 to visit relatives in Newark.

"What do you think? We could do this, couldn't we?" I tried not to jump up and down and wet my pants in front of Cookie.

"We could, but we won't," she said. I was pleased that her hair had been changed to Rod Stewart, *circa* 1970. "Ever hear of liability?"

"I hear the word liability every night on TV," I said, "and it's usually coming out of the mouth of some asshole lawyer. This is about Margaret and giving her a present she'll remember the rest of her life. How often do you have a chance to do that?"

Cookie smiled at me and said, "Every day at lunch. I can do it with an extra Jell-O and never take a patient off the property illegally."

I walked up to her desk, feeling as though I were approaching a judge's bench. When I called the owner of the Paradise Theater, he was all for a private visit and told me we could bring Margaret in on a Thursday or Friday afternoon between shows and have the place to ourselves. I hadn't asked Margaret yet, and typically, hadn't really thought of the legalities.

"Cookie, you know Margaret doesn't mix here. Can you imagine how lonely she must be? What would you want if you were Margaret?"

She wasn't smiling now, and she wasn't exactly Cookie any more, either. She was more like Ms. Smerzz. . . . "I'd want a place that was run with my protection in mind," she said. And that was the end of it.

The next day at Albright High, I was in the middle of another lackluster discussion with my junior class, trying to light a fire under them with "The Great Gatsby." Half of them were gazing out of the window like prisoners and the rest were busy passing notes to each other, the only brush with writing they had this semester without a grimace. Then I tried the old tactic of intercepting a note one student passed to another and reading it aloud to embarrass them. But the note turned out to be so sexually graphic that I wound up choking halfway into the knotted handkerchief segment. The class, of course, was thrilled, and clearly disappointed F. Scott Fitzgerald didn't write like this.

"I just don't think this novel is relevant anymore," my best student, Shirley Jacobson offered, giving her chewing gum such a workout it jingled her earrings.

"Why is that, Ms. Jacobson?" I asked.

"Because gangsters don't drive around in old cars anymore."

Richard Lupo piped up from the back of the class, "Hey, my dad fixes up old cars and drives them around in the Fourth of July parade."

This was where our Gatsby discussion was headed before Julia Finchner bobbed her head inside the door.

"Excuse me, Mr. Pruett, you have a phone message in the administration office."

"Thank you, Julia," I said. As soon as she snapped her

head out of the room, several of the kids starting cracking up. At least a few of them had grasped the concept of irony.

I went to the principal's office to pick up the message from Blanche, the head secretary who resembled Yasser Arafat. She handed me the note as if I'd done something wrong. It was from Cookie, asking me to call her as soon as possible.

"Is that you, Herb?" Cookie asked, her voice crackling over the phone line.

I turned my back on Blanche, trying to indicate that I'd like a little privacy. "Everything all right over there?" I asked Cookie.

"I've been thinking about what you said about Margaret."

"Yes."

"Do you think you can get here in a half-hour or so?"

"Are we going to the movies?" I asked. That got a glance from Blanche.

"I may have to enter therapy soon, but yes, let's take Margaret to the Paradise."

"I'll be there in fifteen minutes," I said.

When I hung up, Blanche sniffed the air and said, "Having any better luck with 'The Great Gatsby,' Mr. Pruett?"

I gave her my best professional smile which fell somewhere between gay and gratuitous and said over my shoulder, "It might not be relevant anymore, Blanche, it's just about gangsters and old cars, anyway."

Margaret and Cookie were waiting for me at the entrance to Albright Manor, so I didn't have the chance to ask Cookie why she had changed her mind, but figured her dueling eyebrows were a good indication she was still not sold on this. Margaret summed it up after we helped her into the front seat of my car.

"We're having an adventure today, Heah-*but*," she said.

I drove through downtown Albright as though I were transporting nitroglycerin and lucked out with a parking spot in front of the Paradise Theater. As we were helping

Margaret out of the car, the owner came out and greeted her.

"Ahh, Mrs. Bowden," he said, "I'm Russell Farrell. How nice of you to visit."

The use of Margaret's last name jarred me, mainly because in all our conversations and mid-afternoon sessions at the piano, I had never known it. She didn't seem like anyone but Margaret to me. Or perhaps Nola.

"I worked for your father, Mr. Farrell," Margaret said, accepting his arm as escort.

"That would have been my grandfather, Mrs. Bowden. You worked for my grandfather."

Cookie and I followed Margaret's slow pace into the theater. The lights were dimmed somewhat, but we could easily make out the great red velvet curtains in front of the screen. We walked halfway down toward the stage when Margaret stopped.

"It's very different from what I remember," she said, "but I know I'm in the same theater. I can hear myself in here. My little spinet was just over there, off the stage."

We began walking down the gradual incline toward the stage, but Margaret stopped again and there was a finality to it. She held her head up in the air as though trying to take in all the ensuing years. We all stood there silently for a moment, and then Margaret started humming under her breath. It might have sounded like heavy breathing to Cookie or the owner of the theater, but I'd heard "Nola" so often, I could recognize its happy melody, even on such a short breath of air.

"We danced right here," she said then, to no one in particular. She turned to face us, her eyes shining with tears. "Thank you, all of you. I couldn't have imagined anything this thoughtful. But I'd like to go back now. I'm getting quite tired."

Margaret's room was small and shiny, with two casement windows that faced the parking lot. The drapes were open and the faculty cars sparkled in the winter sun. I couldn't help but think the view of the automobiles was more optimistic than the Albright Memorial Cemetery. Margaret sat up in bed, the sheet and blanket arranged neatly across her lap. Her hands looked like a pale tangle of spiders. She sighed when she saw me and motioned me to her side.

"Heah-*but*, I could never thank you and Cookie enough for this afternoon," she said. "But I wanted to tell you something. You said I had influence with the music. I've thought about that a bit. You were right, but I also used to play so it *wouldn't* be silent in the Paradise. I'd look behind me and see all those faces flickering in the darkness—silent faces, watching other silent faces. It was too quiet. And now you're doing the same thing with your class. That's influence too, Heah-*but*."

I didn't know what to say. I couldn't remember the last time someone told me I had any influence on anything. Margaret looked tired and I leaned in to give her a hug. She smelled of talcum powder and soap, and when her arms encircled my neck, I was surprised at how strong her embrace was.

And then I felt the tears running down my face before I realized I had started to cry. It surprised me so much that I didn't have time to be embarrassed, and Margaret said softly in my ear, "It's all right. You just go on, everyone needs that. Silences are made to be broken."

After a few moments, I broke our embrace and quickly headed for the door before I collapsed into a caterwauling heap, grieving for everything, from my fucked-up life to the Red Sox to the assassination of Abraham Lincoln. I turned just before shutting Margaret's door and saw her bathed in the rusty light of that afternoon. Her hands were back down on her lap again, but her fingers kept prickling over the folds of the blanket like two crabs exploring a tidal pool, perhaps playing a silent melody.

When the phone rang that following Monday evening, right after the six o'clock news, and Cookie said, "Herb," as though from far away, I knew something bad had happened. We didn't have a call-on-whim relationship yet, though we had gone into Cambridge to the Brattle Theater three times in the past few weeks. They didn't feel like official dates, but they were better than coffee breaks.

The fact that Cookie accepted a second night out with me was miraculous considering the nightmare of our first. I was so nervous about appearing casual and relaxed that I yawned incessantly throughout the film, not very considerate to her or the original "Dracula" we sat through. Later that night, hovering around her face and hoping for a good night peck, I said, "I had a wonderful time, Bunny." Cookie must have had a thing for bumbling charm, because she laughed and told me she'd like to go into Boston next time.

But this phone call was about Margaret. She had fallen Saturday night and badly broken her leg. I shuddered when Cookie compared it to a long piece of chalk.

"There were complications with Margaret's respiration once she got to Albright Hospital," Cookie said. "And then, this afternoon, she just died, Herb. She just died. I'm so sorry to have to tell you like this."

I held the phone tightly to my ear and heard the tinny residue of other conversations trickling through the line. I had been sure Cookie was going to stop at the broken leg. Surely nothing more than that.

"I should be more composed about this than I am," Cookie said. "Look, Herb, it's the nature of this business. We lose someone nearly every week here. It was just Margaret's time."

Cookie allowed me a long silence.

"Do you think the trip to the Paradise was too much for her?" I asked, finally.

"Of course not. It was a wonderful gift from a special person. Don't you dare think that way."

"Margaret had an elderly niece in Wellesley, didn't she?

What's going to happen?"

Cookie was back in charge now, and on familiar turf talking to people about funeral arrangements. "There is a law firm through the niece that is handling those things. I spoke to them a little while ago and Margaret's, ah, remains will be taken to the family plot there."

"But she had nothing to do with Wellesley," I complained weakly.

"Herb. . . ."

My shoulders sagged and I felt as though I had taken a punch. I had run out of things to say, which was nothing new to Cookie.

Over the past couple of months since her death, Margaret had taken up a special residence in my heart. I had no idea what was in that envelope, but my trust in her was so complete that I still felt a reverence toward it. I resisted the urge to pour myself another drink and put the glass in the sink. The water took a few moments to turn hot and, while rinsing, I looked across at the other buildings in my apartment complex. A young girl's head appeared at one of the kitchen windows in the building directly across from mine. She couldn't have been beyond six years of age, and from her reaction, I knew she saw me as well. She gave me a slow, tentative wave, then started moving her arm faster and faster, pretending it was out of control. I laughed and waved back like a fool, flouncing my own arm up and down, until she laughed. Then I picked the glass back up out of the sink and poured myself a half glass more of bourbon and went back to the hall table.

Across the back flap of the envelope someone had written, "Forwarded by Joseph A. Driscoll, Attorney at Law." I forced myself to break the seal slowly, and pulled the yellow lined pages out of the envelope. It must have been extremely arduous to write, the words running off the page occasionally or lapsing into barely decipherable shapes that seemed to ache in their formation. At the top of the first page she had scribbled, "Nola's Story."

Before movie sound came along, I played piano in the theater while the films rolled on the screen. It was so grown-up feeling, taking that trolley down street and walking over to the new Paradise Theater with the velvet curtains and soft chairs. My piano was just off a small stage in the corner. It was a little spinet, old and not tuned very well, but to me it sounded like a concert grand piano. I'd have to crane my neck to see what was happening on the screen, then just play whatever came to mind.

I had learned that nice song Nola when I first started playing and that always seemed to go so well with happy love stories. I played it any time a man and woman were on screen, which was almost all the time. I think the people in the theater might have gotten tired of Nola but no one ever said anything to me, so I just kept playing it.

Something else happened to me at the Paradise. I met my husband there. He used to come to the pictures every Wednesday and after a while, he started to walk down the aisle and stand behind me while I played my Nola song, and then on another day, he put his hand on my shoulder and that old Nola song played right inside my heart.

One afternoon he asked me to dance. I told him I couldn't because I had to keep playing for the movie, but he insisted, and he was so tall and handsome in that silvery light from the screen that I just stood up, and we danced right there in the aisle in front of everyone. What about the music, I asked him, and he started to hum my Nola song in my ear. And so we danced to the Nola that he hummed, and we danced and danced until someone started to clap and soon enough everyone in the theater applauded. It was embarrassing to me and I was afraid of losing my job, but it was the best dance I ever had.

He started to call me his Nola girl, and he would arrive early every Wednesday and make me get up from the piano and waltz in the aisle with him. I loved the way his neck smelled, like cedar, and the way he held me in his arms.

We eventually married, but things started to change almost right away. He didn't want me playing at the Paradise on Wednesdays anymore and no matter how much I begged him, he told me that no wife of his should ever have to work. It wasn't work, I told him, but I could tell he had made up his mind and wouldn't allow me to play at the Paradise anymore.

It got bad for her after that, really bad. This tall handsome man began to hit his Nola girl and still Nola begged him to let her go to the Paradise because her song kept playing over in her heart, but he became more angry every time she asked.

She had two beautiful children, one was a boy named after her husband Robert, who was always sickly and died young, before he was fifteen. Her daughter was named after Robert's mother, but Mildred always sounded so old for a child to carry around with her, and so she tried calling her Nola after her favorite song, but her husband never liked this and made her stop. When Mildred ran off early and married an Army man, Nola wasn't surprised, but felt as alone as if she had been dropped off in the midnight desert. Nola began to know her daughter as an adult through the letters she received, usually twice a month, and maybe a few postcards. She sounded happy then, but eventually the letters dwindled down to a few a year and then just stopped, which seemed somehow worse, even worse than young Robert's death. Nola always wondered why her husband never spoke of it, and then she figured out he had got hold of Nola's letters first and threw them away.

When she asked her husband to fill the awful silence of their home with a piano, he refused. No matter how much money he made or how many times Nola asked, he always said it would lead to no good. Nola reminded him that the piano had led to their marriage, and now that was no good, either, but he ignored her.

As the years went along, it would have been better if Robert had just ignored Nola, but now he hit her a lot, although each time he said it was the last time. He told her he was sorry, and that he was really only mad at the way their lives had turned out. Two nights before Christmas one year, Robert was in a bad car accident and had to stay in the hospital for a few weeks, then in a place where he could try to learn to walk again, but it was not meant to be. Robert couldn't have his legs after that, just like Nola couldn't have her piano.

Those might have been the happiest weeks Nola had, when Robert was away in the hospital. She made a paper keyboard and practiced with it on the kitchen table, humming the notes that she knew would come up from the keys. When they brought Robert home after a while in a special bed, he was worse to Nola than ever.

He didn't have the strength to hit her anymore,

but beat her instead with his words and his hateful looks. Nola went out every morning for his whiskey because that was the only thing that would calm him down, a pint in the morning and a pint in the late afternoon. They lived like that for five months, with him always shouting something terrible at Nola every day. Time had no meaning for her until one morning, after he said something about the children, and then he told her to fluff his greasy pillow. Nola did what he said and then she placed it back on the bed wrong, very wrong, over his face and held it down with her strong piano hands.

I called his doctor and the ambulance, but those nice young men couldn't get Robert to breathe again and then the police came to the hospital and asked me about all those whiskey bottles. I told them the truth. That Robert could never get through the day without them, that it was only what I brought him in the morning and in the afternoon that made him tolerate living. The doctor told them that Robert had still been in very bad condition from his automobile accident for almost half a year now, and he wasn't surprised at his patient's death. There would be no autopsy unless the family wanted one.

We didn't.

I never got the piano I wanted, and after that went to work at the dry cleaners in Natick. I knew I couldn't afford to keep our home, and didn't really care for it that much anyway, so I sold it and moved into a small apartment a block from work. I probably could have bought a small piano then, but I just never got around to it, and time seemed to move me through the years. I felt as though I never touched the sides of life as I passed through. Coming to Albright Manor seemed to happen all of a sudden to me and it's just as well.

And that is the story of Nola you once asked for, Herbert. I know it's not what you expected, but then we'd both agree, neither is life.

Margaret had finally joined our memoir group and I'm still trying to catch up to the encounter. I know how much I miss the music of those afternoons. It seemed to me there was more life consumed in those few minutes than in the balance of my entire week, and now I wonder if Margaret wasn't trying to squeeze a lot of missed life into them as well.

I read through the pages again, slowly imagining her life, every word that ached on those pages. Finally I brought the letter into the kitchen and turned the gas burner on, holding the corners over the wavering flame. After it caught on fire, I dropped it into the sink and looked out the kitchen window. The little girl was there again and her eyes widened when she saw me. We began to wave at each other like flapping ducks.

It suddenly seemed reckless not to take part in life a little more. Perhaps to have a Paradise Dance.

I went back to Albright Manor to finish up the last two weeks of our second workshop, but I knew I was losing steam when I upbraided Mr. Shapiro for his lack of hyphenation in "multi-orgasmic." I knew Margaret was too much a missing part for me to continue there. Then again, it might have been the piano sitting mute in the corner like a spurned friend. It probably should have been more poignant leaving my students, but there was only so much room for that.

And then there's been Cookie. I don't know if she ever saw Margaret's letter, but I've never spoken to her about it.

We have a lot of other things to talk about. Every Wednesday afternoon now, I leave Albright High with great purpose and race home to meet Cookie at my apartment. She brings the Chardonnay and I put on Ben Webster or Vivaldi, depending on her mood. Then we romp around like Lady Chatterley and the gatekeeper. I supply my share of the spark.

Still, whenever I try to introduce her to someone, I get hopelessly entangled in the labyrinth of consonants— *Smerzynski*, can you imagine? And it wasn't that long ago that I found out Cookie's real first name is Leslie. Now that's some intimate knowledge, just like the look of her sleepy face, nuzzling in my arms before work Thursday mornings.

A few weeks ago, I organized a memoir workshop in a rest home out in Framingham. There's a piano there and I indulge myself before every class, plunking a few notes from a tune called "Nola," and try to wrest the melody from the puzzle of keys. I'm getting pretty good at these workshops, and we didn't need a favorite author discussion to get it jump-started.

As it turned out, a few of my new students recognized the melody I was coaxing out of the piano, and then it was really just a matter of allowing the power of their own lives to emerge from the silence.

Oh, Happy Day

"I is another."—Arthur Rimbaud

THEY HAD come to Paris for all the reasons troubled lovers had throughout the centuries. They knew they had to do something out of the ordinary—a travel radical, as Duncan put it—and Paris was it after he read an essay aloud to his wife Helen that concluded, "If you can't find romance in Paris, your heart has died ahead of you, for Paris is the star of your very best dream." Helen loved phrases like that even if they didn't really mean anything. So Paris it was.

Duncan was a struggling painter with limited talent, but he was also a cracker jack Volvo mechanic, which allowed him to hone his mediocrity as long as he kept the will to paint. Helen was a waitress at Pancho's Tacos out on Route 9 in Albright and had some decent upper body strength from schlepping margaritas around in glasses the size of small aquaria. Addicted to aerobics and with more than a passing interest in dance, Helen also knew the second chorus to a lot of songs, which Duncan found so desperately appealing when they first met.

Their marriage counselor, a pinched-faced Kenny G fan who changed her name to Windsong, had been charging them $110 an hour. When she suggested Duncan and Helen start coming twice a week, they went home and did the math and found it was cheaper to go to Paris. The idea was to go there for a month during the summer to find out whether there was any love left in the tank. They rented an apartment on the Right Bank in a quiet neighborhood that overlooked a wine museum, and prepared to dance and paint their way back into each other's hearts.

"This place is French as hell," Duncan said from their balcony window. He craned his neck to see a sliver of the Eiffel Tower between buildings. It was the balcony where Marlon Brando's death scene was shot for "The Last Tango in Paris."

Helen leafed through the *Herald Tribune* and blew a cloud of French tobacco toward Duncan.

"Hon, do we have any butter?" he asked, turning from the window.

"When are you going to start painting?" she asked.

"We just got here. I have to get acclimated." His easel sat in the corner, a tripod of guilt.

"Well," Helen said, throwing the paper aside and jumping to her feet, "let's go get acclimated."

They spent the week riding the Metro and walking the city. Across Boulevard Saint Germain and up and down Boulevard Saint Michel. They fed pigeons in the Luxembourg Gardens and drank espresso that exploded with caffeine in a bistro across from Notre Dame. They looked for their love through the narrow alleys of the Latin Quarter and the sagging bookshelves of Shakespeare and Company. They meandered through the Louvre and were overwhelmed with the everything of it all, so they walked through the cemetery at Père Lachaise, hovering over Gertrude Stein and Chopin and Marcel Proust. They found Jim Morrison's grave by following the sweet tang of hashish, and wound up sharing a pipe the size of a mixing bowl with a half dozen kids born a decade and a half after Morrison's last bath.

Jacked and buzzed, Duncan insisted that he and Helen get drunk at some of Hemingway's favorite haunts—the standards like Le Select, Le Deux Magots, and Le Dôme. At the Select, they waited outside on the chairs for ten minutes before a waiter arrived. When he finally showed up, he looked as though he had just come back from the tallest pompadour in Paris competition and Helen, quick to take offense for bad service after doling out plenty herself for years, said to him, "You know, it wouldn't fluff your hair to give us a little service. What's your story?"

The waiter made a hissing sound and Duncan ordered two brandies and two beers, which he was sure would cost him more than his first car.

"What's Hemingway got to do with painting?" Helen grumbled after the waiter left to go spit into their drinks. Her hat, which had been set at a jaunty angle, had now slumped down over one ear, seeming to defy gravity. The few actual Frenchmen drinking at the café stared at her as though they were selecting a duck for dinner. She felt frisky and winked at one of them.

"Hemingway was a student of painting," Duncan said. "He said all writers should study art in order to understand composition." Duncan leaned back and tried to frame Helen in the meaty chapel of his two hands. This brought a ripple of laughter from the French.

"You're as beautiful as a new watch," Duncan said into Helen's ear. He was still in the throes of hash-love and thought about biting her earlobe.

"It's funny you're not a better painter, Duncan, you certainly have all the secondary moves down pat; you're depressed, you're a drunk, and the only time you want sex is in public."

This wasn't what Duncan wanted to hear, and they both realized they should have toured a cathedral instead of Morrison's grave and Hemingway's watering holes. They had reached the stage in their marriage where they didn't drink well together anymore. The bickering and drinking continued from café to bistro all afternoon. They eventually found themselves at the entrance to the Museé D'Orsay and staggered in. Duncan soon discovered the Realism wing and slumped into a chair to stare at Gustave Courbet's *A Burial at Ornans*, a massive painting measuring some ten by twenty-two feet, dark and foreboding, the entire village turned out to bury one of their own.

Helen, hatless now as a result of tipping her head while trying to view the gargoyles of Notre Dame while standing on the Pont Neuf, plunked down next to Duncan. She pointed her finger at the huge painting across from them.

"Now that's got sadness written all over it," she said. "No guessing what's going on there."

"So you say," Duncan said. "Look at how all the mourners have their faces turned. We don't know if they're sad or not." He looked at Helen and pretended it was for the first time. Yes, he would have fallen in love with her again, with those green eyes and the rusted curls of her summer hair and that full mouth that reminded him of a torn pocket when she was angry. She had a mouth made to speak French. They both stared at the Courbet.

"You want to know the saddest thing I can think of?" Duncan asked.

"Sure, why not?" Helen said cheerfully.

"I never heard my father say, 'I'm happy.' Not once did I ever hear him say that."

Helen rolled her eyes. "Oh, Jesus, men and their daddies," she said. "Always chasing their daddies. You know, Duncan, I've never heard you say that either. And I know I never will. That's the problem with you, there's such a lot of nevers."

She got up slowly and looked at the painting again. "It looks like the whole village is ready to bury itself," she said. Duncan watched her walk away, the dance hidden in her body. He had the uneasy feeling it was for the last time.

Duncan joined the mourners in Ornans and stared at the black, cold hole in the ground they had dug for one of their own. Who was going to bury him if Helen went away? He didn't know how long he sat there staring at the painting, but a guard came up to him and gestured toward the door to indicate closing time. He took one last look at the painting and half expected the grave to be filled in, with his name chiseled in marble above it.

Duncan walked back to the apartment and knew by the sound the key made in the lock that Helen would not be there. He felt a churning in his bowels. All through this rocky marriage he kept thinking that no matter how bad it was, everything would be all right if they hung on long enough. But now, here in Paris, where great romances were launched to last throughout history, he felt helpless over the weakness of their union.

He knew he had to go out looking for her, but where do you look for your wife after dark in the City of Light? He left their apartment and began to walk along the bridge toward the Left Bank. When he came to the peninsula that jutted out into the Seine—the Isle of Swans, he thought he had read—Duncan went down the stairs and began to walk out toward the end of the tree-lined spit of land that divides the Seine.

There were benches on both sides to watch the floating traffic coming up from Honfleur and Rouen. He remembered this was where Beckett and Joyce would meet and talk about their work. Tonight, though, all of the benches had been taken over by couples of indeterminate sex, most of them going at it as though the Germans were due back in town soon.

Toward the end of the island, Duncan was surprised to see a small replica of the Statue of Liberty lit up by a pair of spotlights. He found himself swelling with the notion of Franco-American camaraderie when he heard a panicked voice call out.

It sounded like, "Ooweee."

He ran over to the edge of the water in time to see the head of a man disappearing beneath the shiny black surface of the Seine. Duncan acted instinctively, and plunged into the river without so much as a *sacré bleu*. The shock of the water hit him like bad news and Duncan, no lifeguard even in his daydreams, began flailing himself. It was in mid-flail that his right hand closed around what felt like the man's head. This had a strangely calming effect on Duncan and tugging firmly on the head, as though holding a bowling ball without holes, he began to make his way to the concrete shore of the Isle of Swans.

He felt an instant dread when he pulled the victim out because he seemed to be missing the lower half of his body. Ancient piranha lurking below the surface of history? The severed remains of Seine pollution? But no, Duncan finally realized that the man he had just brought back from black water oblivion was a midget.

"Monsieur," the man sputtered in English, "thanking you for saving my life, but now you please let go of my head."

Duncan released his grip. "How did you know I speak English?"

"No Frenchman would jump into the Seine to rescue anyone, Monsieur" he said. He bowed, an oddly touching gesture from someone so close to the earth and the water drained off both victim and rescuer, pooling at their feet below the base of the Statue of Liberty. "My name is Ouelette and I owe you my life. Did you know, Monsieur, this is the place where the bones of horses and Protestants were dumped five hundred years ago? I am a performer of the avenues and come here to practice my tumbles. I have tumbled too far and now we are very wet."

"Look, I have a place just off the bridge," Duncan said. "We can go there."

Ouelette nodded, but hesitated. "You must know, Monsieur, though I am on the Isle of Swans after dark, I am not what the English call a poof. I cannot engage in sex with a man, no matter it is the man who saved Ouelette's life."

"That should work out OK, Ouelette," Duncan said. "I

am, in fact, looking for my lost wife."

"Ah then," the small man said, brightening. "This will be a perfect Paris evening—tragedy, bravery, a lost love."

Back at the apartment, Duncan loaned Ouelette his robe, which looked like a striped tablecloth on the midget, and put his clothes in the dryer.

"You are an artist, then, Dooncan?" he said pointing at the easel in the corner.

"I thought I was. Until this afternoon. I sat in front of a Courbet too long and now I'm afraid I'm not even a poor pretender."

Ouelette scratched the stubble on his chin and studied Duncan's face. "Well, looking at it the wrong way, you're right, of course. But perhaps I can help you. What if I could show you a way that can make you more important than a mere artist? Dooncan, why be an *artiste mediocre* when you can be great art itself? I will show you."

It was nearly midnight. In the past four hours Duncan had lost the love of his life, rescued a midget from the Seine, giving up painting. A hangover was percolating at the back of his head. But Duncan was a gamer.

"Oui, Ouelette. Mais, oui!" he shouted.

Nothing done well gets done easily. Duncan left the apartment that night and moved into Ouelette's predictably cramped quarters on the rue de Cardinal. Every day for two weeks, Ouelette prepared Duncan to join him on the street. Ouelette was not only a pretty fair tumbler, but a master of makeup and design, and this is where he focused on Duncan, altering his slightly hang-dog face with blotches of clay and a palette of makeup. Then, day after day, hour after hour, in that tiny space above a florist's shop, Duncan learned the techniques of the Queen's palace guards and the great street performers who had gone before him—how to withdraw to a place where nothing could reach you but the art itself. Duncan learned to live quietly in the agonized embrace of perfect stillness. To become, in fact, a cold stone work of art itself.

And so, one bright afternoon three weeks later on the Pont Neuf, the unlikely duo emerged from the shadows of their caps and capes and put on a show for the meandering crowd. Ouelette placed his top hat upside down for contributions and began a tumbling routine that stopped people in their tracks. His little body twisted and turned, he flipped and flew, and people stopped and clapped and threw money into the hat before hurrying along to their precious cafés and busy shops. Duncan sat quietly behind a curtain set over a gilded picture frame held up by a few well placed supports designed by the genius, Ouelette.

When he finished his last set of half-gainers, landing neatly next to the picture frame, Ouelette dramatically drew the curtain aside, announcing, *"Madams et Monsieurs, La Mona Lisa."* And there was Duncan, not just a reasonable facsimile, but the heart beating image of Mona Lisa. She was young and robust, but with the proper gesture towards serenity: the deep set, nearly Asian eyes, a full masculine nose, and then the smallish mouth that looked as though it couldn't pronounce difficult words.

The pedestrians cried out, *"Magnifique!"* *"Mon Dieu, elle est vivante! Bravo, artiste!"*

Money flowed into Ouelette's top hat. Tourists stopped and snapped photos. A crowd began to gather and Ouelette quickly drew the curtain back over Duncan's face. The Mona Lisa needs her rest.

And that is how their mostly triumphant days went. Duncan and Ouelette would set up at different locations throughout Paris, staying a few steps ahead of the police because Ouelette didn't believe in street permits.

Never had Duncan felt such a connection with the mind of an artist as when he sat frozen in time portraying the

Mona Lisa for ten minute stretches. He could almost feel himself being created under da Vinci's hand.

But Duncan knew it was Ouelette who was the master here, and if this can be achieved, why not taste the watery spirit of Monet or flex the peasant muscle of Corot? It would only be a matter of time until Ouelette's great talent and Duncan's dedication would allow him to mix with the mourners at *A Burial in Ornans*. To look down into the maw of that grave and see who was laid to rest.

It was at the busy intersection of rue Saint Jacques and Boulevard Saint Michel a week later. Ouelette had just finished his tumbling flourish and opened the curtain on the Mona Lisa. Duncan was deep within himself, a barely-breathing time-lock of art, wherein he could sense the rustle of Mona Lisa's hair in the breeze of a 15th century afternoon. And so, when he first heard that voice that was once like the sweet ring of a magic chime to him, it nearly made him glance over. Paris is the smallest big city in the world and, of course, it was Helen.

Duncan watched her outline from the periphery of his eye and heard her voice clearly now.

"Isn't it remarkable?" she was saying to the man with her. He was silent, but Duncan sensed that he shrugged.

Helen stepped closer to the picture frame and Duncan could feel her familiar presence; her breath, the working of her jaw, the close fragrance of her body, the Helen-ness that made her as familiar to him as his next breath. The man tugged at her arm, impatient to leave the street performance. But Helen wanted to be held in the grasp of this remarkable sight for just a little while longer, to give in to the strange intimacy she sensed. It was such an audacious public act, and she thought then she understood the complete surrender this portrayal took. It made her want to dance.

The man called her name softly and it sounded like, "Heleeen." As she turned to go, Helen thought she heard something, but it couldn't be. She surveyed the faces around her, but didn't see any clues to what she now doubted she heard in the first place. Though the air was full of the rapid fire French of the Parisians around them, Helen could have sworn someone had whispered into the air that swept across the Seine, "I'm so happy."

A King's Epitaph

"Who doesn't desire his father's death?" — Dostoevski

1.

GIVEN THE rich mahogany that permeated our Victorian house on Walnut Street, the choice of silver for Duke Henderson's coffin was a surprise. A high-tech kind of silver, too, not some Paul Revere affectation. Sleek and shiny like one of his new Lincolns, the mayor's eternal vessel looked as if Martha and the Vandellas could easily erupt from hidden speakers. Not that anyone would have been surprised, given the bombast with which Duke rumbled through life.

I meant to ask Mother about this great silver ship, but the long twisting line of sympathetic characters made it too difficult. Some of them jammed the huge foyer of our house, others ransacked the hors d'oeuvres in the dining room, while the rest lined up outside rehearsing their moments of personal tribute. My father had been the mayor of Albright, Massachusetts, a weary town in the busy maze between Boston and Worcester and a burg squarely on the left-hand page of history. But still, when the mayor of an old mill town like Albright dies, everyone shows up, even some of the Beacon Hill crowd.

I assumed I had been standing at the head of his coffin, but it would be just like my relationship with my father if I had been guarding his feet all afternoon. I walked over to a window and looked out. They were still pouring in, an endless glut of mourners, spilling from their cars in dark suits and hats. The men spoke to each other as they met on the sidewalk, their breaths colliding in back-spinning clouds of crisp November air, while the women waited in chilly patience, wrapped in heavy coats and skins, stabbing through the frost line with their heels into the spongy comfort of the front lawn.

My older brother, Peter, and my mother braved this litany of well-wishers while I was relegated to standing by the coffin to nod at people. There was a lot of nodding going on. I looked around the room, hoping to spot my sister, Sharon, but gave up quickly in the commotion and brought my list out to double-check it.

1. Call Hetzel's Catering re: complaint about sour carrots.
2. Find blue shirt for funeral tomorrow.
3. BOMC sent wrong book.

The family dwelling was a few bedrooms and a couple of baths short of ostentatious, but stepping into the foyer from the front door, a visitor was charged hard by mahogany, especially the polished and majestic sweep of the staircase. Like the excavated steps of a forgotten temple, the staircase rose to the second floor, its dark handrail following the gentle curl of the stairs, while the center of the foot treads were concave from a century of scuffling feet. My father lay at the foot of those stairs, exactly where they placed his father and would have put his grandfather had he bobbed to the surface after drowning off Nantasket Beach.

I watched Mother brush the seat of a chair before sitting. She always did this seat brushing, whether it was at the Governor's house or Burger King, and usually managed it with an air of sophistication. Her beauty was aging gently and she easily seemed 65 or so, ten years younger than reality. Though under 5′ 5″, she gave the impression of height because of her erect carriage and a habit of tilting her head back slightly when she spoke. Her eyes were large and pale blue, and on another person might seem too eager and inquisitive. It was a face wonderfully built on high expectations.

"Oh yes, Mr. Rollins, my husband spoke of you often," she lied brightly to a stranger. Some of Duke's worst enemies came in, compassion applied to their faces like stage makeup, but Mother smiled through all this tedium. And while I long ago stayed out of his politics and his way, I was sure a lot of these characters were what Duke would have called the *fuck-ees*.

"Gilby," he said to me twenty-five years ago at my high school graduation, "there are in life the *fuck-ees* and the *fuck-ers*. You better figure out which side you want to be on."

Then, almost as an afterthought, he gave me an old Toyota.

There was a part of me, beyond the mingled sadness and fury I had for him, that was embarrassed it was *our* father who died; Duke—the Great Accommodator, the Titan of the Turnpike Extension, a man the Governor recently described as the "Mayor of Massachusetts." Death seemed like such an unimaginative insult to the vast life of Joseph "Duke" Henderson. Maybe it was a failure of God that Duke simply died like all the mortal men.

"Gilby," Peter muttered urgently at me from the other end of the casket, "Gilby, do you think you could get Mrs. Belfort a glass of water?"

Mrs. Belfort, a known event-fainter, leaned into Peter's large blue suit. She looked ready to go so I headed for the kitchen: Gilby, the middle child, fetcher of water, named after a misplaced relative for a long-forgotten kindness. If not the black sheep, surely a spotted one.

My sister, Sharon, was in the kitchen, standing by the sink, staring dreamily out the window. She sloshed a half glass of Scotch around.

"I need to get Mrs. Belfort some water," I said to her.

"Didn't she faint at your high school prom?" she asked. Sharon was forty-one that year, two years my junior and pretty in a 1940's movie star way. She had long auburn hair that swept across her forehead and a jagged smile that ended abruptly at the corners of her mouth.

"I think you're right," I said. "She keeled over during *Harlem Nocturne*."

Sharon turned to look out the window again, bumping up against the sink with her stomach. "I would have liked to have seen him once more. How come the coffin's closed?"

I filled a large glass with water. "I don't know, probably something Mother told me Duke said to her years ago. He came home one night from a wake and told her that when he died he wanted the lid closed because he didn't want anyone staring at him if he couldn't stare back."

"And how come silver?"

"Hi-ho." I shrugged.

"God, it looks like a nuclear device. Mother seems to be doing fine, though."

I nodded. "Yeah, she's glad we all made it home."

Sharon scrunched her face at me. "Jesus, Gilby, Daddy *died*. You think I'm going to call Mother and tell her I can't make it, I got other plans? Massage? Yoga?"

"I didn't mean it that way. I think she's just glad to have everyone under one roof, that's all. Peter's not around much, with his monster car dealership, you out in Springfield, and me doing my sensitive art restorer act."

Mrs. Belfort arrived, pale-faced and staggering into the kitchen with Peter propping her up from behind.

"Christ's sake, Gilby," he hissed desperately, "what about the goddamn water!"

I handed Mrs. Belfort the glass and it went right through her hand as though greased on all sides, shattering explosively on the linoleum floor.

"Fucking hell!" Peter yelled, jumping back. It was a hearty invective appropriate to the destination of many of the people in the house and it occurred during a particularly quiet time in the foyer, so it rang out quite well for all to hear.

Mrs. Belfort wavered, coughed and fluttered her eyes. Color dawned on her ashen cheeks.

"Some water got dumped on her feet," I said to Peter. "It was pretty cold. Might have helped, actually."

Peter handed Mrs. Belfort over with a nudge from his hip. "Gilby, I have to get back to the line. There's State House people coming in who Mother might not know. Maybe you could handle *this?*"

Besides looking a lot like him—the big honker and bald pate—Peter had Duke's lavishness and was excellent at minimizing other people's tasks while aggrandizing his own. I gave him the aw-shucks smile. He stopped at the kitchen door and looked at us. He had Duke's height, too, they both always seemed a bit taller than anyone else in the room.

"We should have held this at the funeral home," Peter said, his voice softening. "We're really not prepared for people fainting or a line of traffic that goes up to Oak Road."

"Duke was a popular guy," I said, adjusting Mrs. Belfort on my hip.

Peter stalked out of the kitchen, his rubber soled shoes yipping on the wood floor of the adjoining dining room. I helped Mrs. Belfort droop into a kitchen chair and Sharon slid a glass of Seagram's under her nose, which made the old girl's eyes widen in interest.

"That's really his first hissy fit," Sharon said. "Peter's been wonderful for Mother. A fucking rock. And he's got Duke's memory for names, too. I stood behind him for a while in that ghoul's line. When he got stumped for names a few times, he made such a big deal of it, the people felt like they'd been complimented instead of forgotten. And his kids? C'mon, he and Eleanor must beat them regularly, they're so good."

Mrs. Belfort leaned over, inhaling the aroma from the

glass. She picked it up and sipped tentatively, then smacked her lips and poured the thing back like a fur trapper. She stared at us. I tried matching her, but you don't easily stare down people in their eighties. That can become their *only* thing to do.

"Feeling better, Mrs. Belfort?" I asked.

"I never felt bad," she sniffed. "Just faint."

We were all quiet for a moment, mulling the difference.

Mrs. Belfort drained her glass and struggled to her feet. "That's all I needed," she said. "Just some fresh air. Thank you."

She waddled out of the kitchen and I followed closely behind in case she did a header by the coffin, but there was some whiskey stamina to her step now. and she bulled her way back into the maelstrom with gathering momentum.

By late afternoon, the line near Mother dwindled and the remaining crowd broke into small cliques. Peter was back at the other end of the coffin, speaking casually to Phil Robertson and a few other members of the Albright Town Council while his elbow rested on the coffin as though he were about to order a martini.

I went over to Mother. "Feeling all right?"

"I haven't smiled this much and not meant it since Duke came in third in the governor's primary," she muttered.

She brushed at a spot on my lapel, then hugged me quickly, and when we drew apart she dabbed at her eyes with the back of her hand.

"You should wear a suit more often, Gilby," she said, "You look positively distinguished."

"I look like a clerk in a cheap shoe store," I said, smiling and looking over her shoulder at Peter. He had draped himself over the box now, outlining some business strategy that required him to trace his fingers along the coffin. Tiny squeaks escaped from under his fingertips while he forged his way along the silver luster, making not only his point, but two hammy streaks in the sheen.

"Negotiating by *not* negotiating . . . ," he said to his rapt audience, this time a new set of assholes from the local Kiwanis whose most recent negotiations were with a bartender.

"It was almost unmanageable, this turnout," Mother said. "Old Chief Sylvester told me he's never seen anything like it before, cars backed up nearly to Route 9. Leave it to Duke, huh? An Albright-wide traffic jam. He would be *very* happy with this."

I envisioned the yawning hole in the ground at Albright Memorial Cemetery that awaited my father, then looked over at Peter again. He wedged a finger sandwich into the left side of his face, then continued lecturing out of the right.

"Peter is very much like Duke, isn't he?" Mother said, proudly. "Look how engaged those men are listening to him. He might not be saying much, but just like Duke, he makes it seem important."

"I hope he doesn't challenge anyone to tic-tac-toe on the coffin," I said.

Peter shook hands with the men and clapped one on the back, raising a small squall of dust particles that tumbled through a slab of afternoon sun; another funeral, another appearance for that guy's suit. He walked them to the door and shut it behind them, one of the few times the front door had been closed all afternoon. We could see our breaths in the foyer.

"Peter, I think it's time we took our house back," Mother said to him, nodding at the remaining groups huddled near the empty serving dish in the dining room. Peter gave a thumbs up and headed for the dining room. His voice had the same resonance as Duke's and boomed over the room like an echo in search of a comeback.

"We're going to wrap it up, folks," he said to them.

Mother winced slightly.

"You're right," I said to her. "Just like Duke.

2.

We endured the final affirmations of grief and when the front door closed again, it seemed to seal us all up in a great silence. Mother and Peter went into the dining room, while Dick Edwards, the funeral director, grabbed my arm on his way out the door.

"I'll leave the keys," he said.

"Keys to what?"

"The coffin. It's unlocked. Shall I just lock it and give Peter the keys? It's customary for the family to keep the keys."

Fucking ghoul.

I didn't know anything about key etiquette, but looking at him reminded me of the story Duke told us one night, that when Dickie Edwards' aunt died, Dickie personally did the prepping of her body.

"Sure, Dick," I said. "I'll keep them. Thanks for everything."

He gave me the funeral director's smile. "I had a great deal of respect for your father. See you tomorrow for the burial?"

"Duke and I'll be there," I said.

He took short choppy steps as if he had a jar of formaldehyde jammed up there and shut the front door behind him. Through the door between the dining room and the kitchen, I could see Sharon splashing dishes in the sink with Peter's wife, Eleanor. Their two kids, a nine year old boy and a seven year old girl, sulked in the corner of the foyer, bored beyond belief by Grandpa's death.

I stuck my head into the kitchen. "I'm going to walk down to Reggie's for a pack of cigarettes," I said, and it seemed to startle everyone.

"Lemme grab my coat and drive you," Peter said.

"That's OK, it's just a few blocks," I said.

Peter stabbed his arms into his coat. "Gilby, I *know* where the hell Reggie's is. I lived here for forty-six years, remember?"

"Every minute of it," Sharon said from the sink and we all laughed, even Eleanor who can be a little tight-cheeked in the humor department. It always seemed to me that Peter's wife felt our family was funny, but not humorous. But then it dawned on me I hardly knew Eleanor, or, for the past five years, any of my remaining family.

My divorce had been especially messy and, being Duke's son, a lot more public than I would have preferred. My darling Rachel, whom I promised so much to during our wedding vows, reminded me one day that I hadn't lived up to one, including the continuing bad habits of drinking, smoking pot, and listening to too much Coltrane. On her side of the ledger, I was pretty sure fucking her old high school honey, now the manager of the Red Roof Inn on Rt. 9 in Natick, violated something, though I had to admit she never promised me she wouldn't do that.

That little affair of hers went on for a couple of years and I imagined they might well have used all 110 rooms available. I do have to give Rachel some credit for restraint since she told me that she turned down Duke's advance one night at an Elks fundraiser. Thanks, Dad. Call me old-fashioned, but it pissed me off that Duke tried to fuck my wife.

The fact is, I was no go-getter and never had been. All those genes had been carefully placed inside my brother and coaxed out by my father. If my mother hadn't seen something in me that the rest of us didn't, I might have drifted off to an ashram outside Denver somewhere, but instead she insisted I developed my fondness for art history. Where my passion for 19th century French realism came from, I don't know, but there is a bit of Duke Henderson in Gustave Courbet, so maybe it was a way of looking at my father without him telling me how to do so. After a few lackluster semesters at Northeastern, I fell into painting restoration.

Once outside, I talked Peter into walking and we set off at a comfortable pace. Three inches shorter than his 6' 2", I couldn't match his long stride, but I also didn't have to match that extra thirty-five pounds, much of it rolling around his belt. I walked a little faster.

Peter adjusted his gait and moved up next to me. "You need anything?" he said finally, puffing slightly through ruddy cheeks.

I didn't answer and waved to old Matt Valentine who clattered by in his rusted Ford wagon. Peter kept his head down and for a moment I wondered if we might break into a jog.

"Why would you ask me a question like that?" I puffed. "Do I need anything?"

Peter's breathing picked up. "I meant I've got a little cash if things are tight in the conservatory business."

"That's conservation, Peter."

"Whatever."

He nudged the pace up a half step and though the late November air drilled us with a sharp chill, I could feel a few beads of sweat meandering down my spine. My breathing started to rattle then, a wheezing from the depths of my throat as though I had just swallowed a whistle.

"Since when have you ever. . . ," I had to stop to breathe, "had to subsidize my living?"

This last phrase cost me valuable oxygen. But Peter was laboring too, sucking in great volumes of air and expelling them through pursed lips that flapped together horsily when he exhaled. My own breathing came out in short raspy sounds and, to keep up with Peter's giant strides, I nearly doubled my own steps. We finally turned up Oak Road and

Reggie's Groceria was in sight.

I heaved a breath at Peter. "I haven't had an allowance since I was fourteen."

I pressed the pace until just short of a trot, figuring that to begin running would be an unspoken violation, like a trotter breaking stride. Peter picked up his feet and slammed them down relentlessly as though on a forced march, his heels making deep indentations in the soft shoulder of the road. Soon the undeclared race broke into full heat, Peter taking a short lead by virtue of his long legged grip of the earth. The back of my head pounded and cold air raked my throat.

Thirty feet from Reggie's doors, Peter slowed and began limping slightly. Charley horse? That's what they always say. He let out a long whoosh of air that raised a brief but great cloud in front of his face as though he might magically disappear behind his own smoke. It startled an overweight woman in tight jeans who overreacted by veering her shopping cart sharply to the left, nearly tipping it over.

"Jerkoffs," she sneered at us.

Peter arrived at the door two steps ahead of me, and then we both leaned against the building, sucking up vast shares of air.

"I think I better take up smoking," Peter panted, "It seems to help."

"You ain't no pulling guard for Albright High anymore, Pete."

I always thought my brother was a more reasonable version of Duke and now, balding and enlarged as Duke had been in his late forties, he seemed even more so. We stood there for a while, huffing and wheezing, still trying to get accustomed to each other in mid-life. I felt as if I should have said something then, anything, to recognize the moment, but I just looked at my shoes. The fact was, we couldn't have been more different and still stay in the same phylum.

177

It wasn't always so. I can remember a time in my early teens when I wanted to be just like Peter. Though somewhat oafish at sports, Peter had enough bulk and ass to start for Albright High's football team. This was important to Duke because in his day, he was like fucking Red Grange on the gridiron. That's how Duke always referred to the football field—the gridiron. Peter could bring off a reasonable rendition of Duke, but it was always distilled.

"Look, I think we should talk about Mother," Peter finally said, his breathing nearly even. He collected the sweat from his brow with a crooked finger and snapped it to the ground where it made a trail on the sidewalk.

"You might think about a salad bar, there, big boy. Doing Jackson Pollocks off your brow after a short walk to the store."

"Don't start with the smart shit, Gilby. We gotta talk sometime about this. All our lives are going to be different with Pop dying."

"Actually, I thought I might move back into the house for a few months. Help Ma sort things out," I said, surprising myself since I hadn't thought of it until just then.

"Gilby, Ma should be able to do what she wants now. Get around a little. You know what I'm saying?"

I looked my brother over and wondered if I would buy a used car from this man. "We have plenty of time for this conversation," I said. "Mother can do whatever she likes. What do you think, I'm going to be laying down some laws or something? Be in by nine, Ma? Don't date guys in the insurance industry?"

An attractive blonde woman with a small child came out of the store and stepped around us, postponing any reply from Peter. I watched his eyes drift openly over her and she met his gaze bluntly, the hint of a flirtatious smile tugging at her mouth. Peter sucked in his stomach and ran his fingers through the sidewalls of remaining hair. He turned his head because, like Duke, his strong thick nose had greater effect if viewed in profile. But the moment passed and we both watched the friendly creases her ass made in her hip pockets while she walked to her car.

Peter turned back to me. "Ah, what was it you were saying, Gilby?" he asked.

3.

Plunging a taco chip into the bowl of salsa on the middle of the dining room table and dribbling a tomato and onion trail to his mouth, Peter seemed right in place sitting in Duke's customary chair at the head of the table. Mother leaned forward and sipped at her coffee mug. It was decaf and Irish Mist, about half and half. I'm sure of the proportions because I mixed it. Sharon had switched to south of the border and now idled over the dwindling Tequila bottle, forsaking the salt and lime ritual three drinks ago, and swirling straight Cuervo in her glass like a bored chemist.

"It had a special meaning, having Duke's wake here, Ma," Peter said. "A very special meaning."

Peter stopped short of actually defining what that very special meaning was and took a long swig of beer, thunking the bottle down on the dining room table. No coaster, I noticed. He sat with Eleanor draped moon-faced on his arm, her spring finally wound down after tucking the kids in and explaining to them it's okay to sleep in the same house with a dead man as long as it's Grandpa.

"Honey, wouldn't you like the least little bit to drink? Beer? Wine?"

Eleanor shook her head and made a face as if Peter had suggested an extra spoonful of Castor oil. Mother started to say something, then cut herself off and drank more of the coffee. Sharon spun the cap off the Tequila bottle and poured herself another three fingers. I might have appeared a little more propitious with my goblet of Cabernet Sauvignon, but the truth is my right foot was asleep and I could no longer say "roory" words like *diary* or *dreary*. We were all, Eleanor notwithstanding, in various stages of drunkenness, including Mother who was fond of a drink, but didn't like drinking.

I pulled a piece of paper out of my pocket and looked at it, the inveterate list maker:

1. Call re: the Acardi painting.
2. Duke/cemetery.
3. Toyota-Wednesday tune up.

Then I got hung up on watching Eleanor's brow, which was always in some stage of wrinkle as if she never could figure our family out. She once asked me why Peter wasn't interested in politics. Clearly she hadn't been satisfied with Peter's answer, and I knew she wouldn't be happy with mine, either. The fact was that Peter never became Duke because he didn't have enough Dukeness in him. Given the right circumstances, I'm sure Peter would have been thrilled to go into politics. But Duke used to brag that what Curley was to Boston, he was to Albright, and while Peter had all of Duke's motions, he had none of the moves. There would be no successor to Hizzoner in the remaining Henderson family. To his credit, Peter recognized that fact early in life, though it still served as a great disappointment to *both* him and Duke.

The fatty I had rolled a few hours ago was burning a hole in my pocket, so I decided to go outside for a smoke and leave Eleanor to continue her confused blinking at us. I went through the kitchen and out the back door to sit on the steps. It was a cruel cold for November and I was glad for any dead man not to have to have to spend at least *this* harsh night in the ground. I lit up and took in a robust lungful.

Sharon opened the door and joined me on the steps.

"Give me a hit of that," she said, sitting next to me. "I love smoking in cold weather, it always seems like you're getting more for your money."

We were silent for a while, and I could hear Peter and Eleanor laughing over something and then someone, probably Mother, clattering around in the kitchen.

"Gilby, I think Mother should sell the house," she said suddenly.

"That's good."

"I mean it. This house. This house is *all* Duke. Whenever I come back here now, I feel like I can never catch my breath."

Sharon took two more hits, then lit a cigarette.

"Let me get this straight," I said. "You live in Richmond, Virginia but this house suffocates you the few times you visit, so you think Mother should sell it. That about right?"

"Not based on that, no. Of course not. I want you to be happy, too."

"Thanks. I am."

She looked at me in the cold darkness. "You'll have to pardon me, Gilby, but I don't think you're any more of an expert on happiness than I am. Mister mystery man these past few years. Christ, you lived six miles away and barely saw Ma or Duke."

I took a hit that would have impressed a reggae singer. "That's just not true. I saw Ma at least once every couple of weeks."

"And Duke?"

"I guess it's inappropriate with him lying thirty feet away, but fuck Duke. He wasn't a father to me since I got too old to be cuffed around. Which, I'd remind you, wasn't until I was nearly thirty."

She stabbed the cigarette out with the arrow of her heel and it sounded like someone knocking at a door. There was no malice in what she said about my visits to the house, just a Tequila truth that tumbled out of her mouth. Mrs. D'Allen-sandro's German shepherd barked deeply from two houses down the street.

Sharon leaned over and kissed my cheek. "I guess none of us turned out perfect, did we?"

"No," I said, "I guess not. But it wasn't like we had the best example for a father, either."

She stood up. "I'm not going to blame Duke all my life for what stinks in it now. By the way, where was that lovely ex-wife of yours?"

That term *ex-wife* always made me feel like one of the guys, something I clearly wasn't. "I talked to her earlier today. She's gracing us at the cemetery tomorrow."

"Big of her."

"Don't waste your ammo on such an easy target. It doesn't matter, she's a non-factor."

Sharon shook her head. "I dunno. 'Cuz I'm drunk, I guess, but wouldn't it be nice to get a second chance on all this? Shit, I'm going inside, it's too cold out here."

When she yanked the door open, Peter's voice rolled out to us sounding very much like Duke.

"Hey, you two, come in here a sec," he yelled from the dining room.

Everyone had a glass in front of them. Mother toyed with some wine now, slogging it around in a circle. She wasn't much of a wine drinker and looked disappointed her coffee was gone. Eleanor stared straight through her glass of red, apparently mesmerized by the sight of her crimsoned hand on the other side.

Peter stood, waving his beer in front of him. "I just want to, uh," he nodded his head vigorously toward the wall that separated the dining room from the foyer and Duke's casket. "Well, you know . . . to Pop. To Duke." He nodded his head once more and tilted the bottle to his mouth. I heard a faint click as the bottle bumped his front teeth.

"To Duke," I said.

"Duke."

"Daddy."

"To Joseph."

We fell silent long enough to make everyone uncomfortable. Sharon cleared her throat and glanced at Peter. Eleanor sighed a meaning-laden, "We-l-l." I thought over a few Duke anecdotes, but nothing seemed very appropriate; the ones I knew all showed what a shit he was.

"It's colder in Albright than Springfield," Peter finally said. "You wouldn't expect it."

"No, I suppose not," Sharon said.

More quiet, the breeding ground for banal conversation. Peter's watch bleated at the top of the hour and Eleanor jumped slightly, then started clearing up the extra glasses, cups, and empty Tequila bottle.

"Eleanor's always a big help," I said, trying to look on the bright side.

Mother sat up straight in her chair. "Listen, all of you. He was my husband and your father and he loved all of us. If he was perfect, they would have called him Duke Christ." She looked at each of us. "And I *know* that the last thought he had was of his family. Me. All of us." Her voice quavered slightly.

Given the circumstances, I doubted Duke's last thoughts were of all of us, but who knows where a mind might wander while pressed between the steamy thighs of a red-haired cocktail waitress named Josephine.

Peter went over and hugged Mother. She seemed so tiny in his arms.

"Of course it was, Ma," he said, and seemed to be crying softly himself now. "His very last thought."

I glanced over at Sharon and saw her eyes filled with tears. I knew the meagerness of my grief isolated me from the rest of the family and I felt as though I had missed something important, an inside secret that was my responsibility to grasp. Sharon went to Mother's side and walked with her into the foyer, Peter and Eleanor following hand in hand. I watched them through the doorway as they paused in front of the coffin, then I cleaned off the rest of the table. By the time I ran everything through the dishwasher and shut off the kitchen and dining room lights, the house was quiet, with Mother settled in an empty room she had shared for forty seven years with my father.

Just before climbing the stairs, I walked over to Duke's coffin. The hall light splashed off the heavy varnish. The streaks Peter left on the surface were still there, meandering down the side. I wished for a wave of sadness to overtake me then, and stood weaving slightly in place, perfectly willing to give myself up to it. Nothing came because nothing was there. I climbed the stairs slowly, each step creaking its own tune under my feet.

The graveside service was short and sweet, unlike the guy they were burying. Mother managed to make nearly everyone cry when she talked for a minute about their early life together. Phil Robertson said a few things about how Duke had always made Beacon Hill pay attention to Albright. I got the distinct notion Robertson was testing the mayoral waters before the body in front of him was scarcely cold.

My ex, Rachel, arrived late, in a cloud of fussing and White Linen perfume, and got just the right amount of attention she always needed. She blew me a kiss from across the grave, which nearly made me laugh until I wondered if perhaps it had been meant for the coffin. She squeezed out a few tears, and knowing Rachel as well as I did, it made me wonder again if maybe she was crying over a lost opportunity instead of a late ex-father-in-law.

Rachel deftly avoided my mother after the ceremony, but told me to extend her deepest sympathy. Then she was off,

off to Rachel World and all its daily surprises and, as it was each time we saw each other, I wondered whether this would be the last time.

It was quiet on the porch in the late afternoon, especially after I quit jiggling my nervous leg against the base of a table. Peter and Eleanor packed the car while I tried in vain to interact with their children. We were on the Adirondack chairs. They looked at me with polite sympathy but did little more than grunt or groan a few responses toward me. When my mother came out I saw the relief flood into their faces. Bonding with Uncle Gilby had come to an end.

"I guess that's it," Peter said, slapping his stomach as he clomped up the front steps. It seemed now as though Duke had died years ago. Eleanor and the kids gave me a peck on the cheek, Peter shook my hand tightly, then hugged me awkwardly, drumming his affection onto my back. The smell of rum mingling with his Aqua-Velva gave him a pleasant island-like redolence. I was happy for Peter that he was into the sauce early today. It would make the drive home to Springfield much better. And faster.

"I'm only a phone call away," he began.

"I know, Peter. Thank you."

Sharon hugged me a couple of times and as the family began to back off the porch, Mother came over and put her arm around me. All of our embracing left a blended Henderson fragrance rising from my clothes and face.

Sharon made a comic gesture—half bow, half curtsy—and stepped off the porch, walking over to Peter's car. She was hitching a ride to the Worcester airport with them. Peter and Eleanor followed, herding the kids into their cabin cruiser Lincoln, the automobile of choice for the Henderson clan, except, of course, Jap-driving Gilby.

"Remember, Gilby, anything you need," Peter yelled. "And thanks for Pop's suits, Ma."

I waved my hand in thanks, still wondering what it might be I needed. As Peter and Eleanor pulled out of the driveway, the kid's faces popped up in the back window, joined by Sharon. We all had our hands in the air in mid-wave when little Joey picked up the arm of one of Duke's pinstripe suits. He waved the empty sleeve at us, up and down and side to side. And just when Peter eased the car out onto Oak Road for the Mass Pike, it seemed for all the world as though Duke was in the back seat waving his final hearty goodbye to us. To those staying behind in Albright.

4.

Mother and I finished the last remains of funeral food in the den that night, airing our gripes aloud at the nightly news. She sat in the striped wingback and I sprawled on the couch with a paper plate of ham, turkey and cheese rising and falling on my stomach. I had smoked most of a joint the size of a White Owl a half hour ago and knew the sandwich would still be rising and falling in a few minutes, this time inside my stomach.

"Comfortable?" she asked me.

"I guess so. Yes. Why?"

She shook her head. "No reason. You just look like you could be in a hammock under a coconut tree."

Dan Rather described a death row execution in Georgia— Ma always over-pronounced it, *Jawja*. When Dan moved to the increase in the federal gas tax, I was all for it.

"Go ahead," I said to the TV, "Spend some on the environment." My five year old Honda Civic—29 mpg city, 34 highway, thank you—sat smugly out in the driveway.

The gas tax inspired a stunning announcement from Mother.

"I don't want Duke's Lincoln to sit there gathering

186

widow's dust," she said to me, aiming the remote so the sound fell back into the TV. "I want you to show me how to drive."

I looked back at the television and saw a reporter hunched over his microphone trying to speak into the face of a gusting wind. He seemed to be overcompensating for the weather, mouthing his words with great deliberation while palm trees whipped and bent in the background. A strong gust caught his upper lip, making him resemble Elvis for a moment.

"Why do you want to learn how to drive at seventy years of age?" I asked feebly.

She sniffed. "Sixty nine years of age. You've been smoking pot again, haven't you?"

"Seventy in three weeks. And no, I haven't been smoking pot again, I've never stopped since high school." I noticed she didn't ask me to *teach* her to drive, only to *show* her how. I took this as a dangerous sign.

"I think people should be able to learn how to drive any time they want," Ma said. "Look at all those old fools you read about in the paper. Some eighty year old woman flying a single engine plane to Nova Scotia for an Oyster Festival, stuff like that. Dan Rather has those stories all the time. I just want to use the car now. I don't want it sitting there like one of Duke's lawn jockeys."

She turned the television back up and changed the subject. "Peter took most of your father's clothing. When he tried on your father's suit jacket he looked *so* like Duke twenty years ago."

We were both quiet after that, the news of an upcoming telethon rattling through the TV at us. And then I heard Mother take her breath in sharply. She started crying then, softly at first and tentatively, as though probing the depth of her own sorrow. I moved over to the chair and put my arm around her, but that only seemed to set her off more. Ma was always shy about crying and covered her face now, her shoulders trembling slowly while a low, soft moan feathered out from between her fingers.

My utter uselessness frustrated me and I couldn't think of anything else to do but pat her on the back and chant the mantra, "It'll be OK, Ma. It'll be OK."

I could fix a pizza stain on the Mona Lisa's head, but couldn't help my own mother to her rightful place of grief.

"It'll be OK."

She cried for a few more minutes, each rack of her body as painful to me as if wrenched from my own heart. After a while, she straightened her back and looked at me through reddened eyes.

"I'm sorry you didn't know the Duke I did, Gilby," she said. "Or at least the great good in him. He used to say that every family has its tragedy. I wonder if he didn't underestimate this family when it came to the tragedy of the two of you."

"People live through sorrow and tragedies," I said. Plato Gilby.

She forced a tired smile and then reached over and ran the back of her two fingers along the line of my jaw. "I guess none of us *really* know each other the way we would design it, do we?"

I felt my face heat up. In truth, had I not loved her so much and felt such a strong sense of protection toward her, I would have been sorry she didn't know the Duke *I* had known.

She stood, then leaned down to kiss me goodnight. "Thank you for everything, dear."

"I didn't do anything, Ma. I haven't done anything all week. I'm sorry for that."

She dismissed me with a wave of her hand and stopped in the doorway to the foyer. "The house feels cavernous, doesn't it?" she said, and before I could answer I heard her footsteps rasp and creak on the stairs.

I sat there for a while, the nearly muted television flickering in a silver monotony. Finally, a bottle of Dewar's seemed to wave at me from under the stereo, and I got up for a glass of ice.

I looked at the wall clock that the Ladies Auxiliary Club awarded to Duke for spearheading the opening of an animal shelter in Albright—a real hoot in our family because we were never allowed pets as kids. Duke always thought dogs and cats were "groveling little beggars that specialized in shit." After the second drink I wouldn't care about replenishing the ice and the third drink would take care of any that lingered in my glass. I'll grieve my own goddamn way.

I shot the TV off with the remote and the den settled into a silent humming. The quiet was too loud. I reached over and snapped the stereo on and plugged in the headphones. While the earphones cupped my ears with its secret music, I inhaled the bitter jolt of that first drink, then shuddered.

Someone had been listening to an Ella Fitzgerald CD and now her voice came through clear and young with that coquettish inflection, singing *Shiny Stockings*. I took another drink, this one paved and prepared for.

Life is a victory reserved for the living, I figured. Don't kid yourself about dying nobly or leaving your mark. And while my life still ticks under my shirt, I can take a brush and solvent and fix the world. Imperfections: aging, cracking, leaking, fading, bleeding. Gilby, literally a doctor of the arts.

In a short while, my glass needed a refill. Duke owned all the life in this house until now. His big-footed ambiance, his broad fearful back, those hale sausage fingers, that inevitable grip. The Scotch swirled around a small raft of ice and bumped gently on my lip when I titled the glass. How would the masters handle all this business on canvas?

I poured myself another and closed my eyes, slipping into

the confident timbre of Ella's voice. She began to scat while the trio fell into a shuffle rhythm and her uncluttered sound rose and fell with the melody, urging the music on, then falling back again. Mental notes:

1. Show Mother how to drive.
2. Help pick out a headstone.
3. Forget the first half of your life.

When I knocked the bottle of Scotch off the table onto the rug, my first concern was wasting nearly half a fifth, then I worried about a refill. I sopped up what had spilled and went down into the cellar where I knew they kept the backup booze. In my family, running out was as *verboten* as running away.

Next to Duke's liquor locker was a filing cabinet that had been in the cellar since I was a child. It was usually locked, but the few times I went through it in childhood snoopiness, I become bored by the papers with tedious language that were always crammed in there. More out of nostalgia than purpose, I yanked on the top drawer and nearly fell over from the thrust when it opened. Inside was the usual scatter of papers, and then I noticed what looked like a pack of letters in the back of the drawer, held together with an elastic band.

Normally I pass over Henderson memorabilia, those cardboard boxes and albums that are lined up in the attic like silent curators, filled with our pictorial and written history. But I was in the cellar now, a place for secrets, already drunk, and halfway through this inescapable night, filled with foreboding—Duke's first night out on the moors. After pouring myself another half glass from the new bottle, I dragged out the letters and flicked the dust balls off.

The envelopes were a light blue, perhaps thirty in all, held together by a dry and cracked rubber band that snapped immediately when I tried to ease the letters out. They were all addressed to the same man, a Mr. Arthur Mirren, not a name familiar to me. But the handwriting was. That dignified capital *M* and those long swirling *r*'s, the sternly crossed *t* and the faintly encircled dot of the *i*. I could picture the roll of the pen under Mother's unmistakable hand. The letters felt intimate even without a reading, tucked so neatly into their envelopes with the stamp and postmark carefully removed, and when I was a few paragraphs into the first one, I knew my mother would be reinventing herself in my mind.

> Dear Arthur,
> I have just enough time to share this lonely
> moon with you and kiss the worry from your
> brow. We will have time, we will. We will find
> each other in the corners of our days and I will
> visit you there and hold you in my arms and
> draw you to me. I love you, my darling, for
> what. . . .

I stopped reading and took a shaky drink, my teeth clattering on the rim of the glass. My palms had become hot and moist. I took the letters upstairs with me. I eased myself onto the couch and put Ella back over my ears. Might as well give the lovers some music.

And then I read them all. Every last flowing syllable, every double-entendre, every yielding paragraph, and every acquiescent comma—I drank them all as greedily as the Scotch. I joined them in hotel cocktail lounges and corner cafés, browsed the rickety shelves of used book stores with them in search of a worn copy of Rimbaud. I strolled with them on their romantic walks in the Back Bay, in the Public Gardens, or the cemetery along Tremont Street. In the fall, there were piles of leaves and the rough wool of carnal daydreams. I eavesdropped on their whispered promises, felt the warmth of their mingled breath, and blinked at the spoony casualness in which they offered their bodies.

> Dearest,
> What you said to me last night bears
> some thought, but we can't forsake everything
> in our lives, either. For now we will have to be
> content that we've found something wonderfully
> unexpected and. . . .

It took me over an hour and half, with plenty of time out for wall staring and drink refreshening. I couldn't help but feel as though Duke was reading over my shoulder, too. When I finished the last letter I put it back into its envelope, dug a new rubber band out of a drawer and put everything back down cellar into the filing cabinet.

The next thing I knew, it was around seven in the morning, the silent cups of the earphones were still in place and the soldiers of white noise marching through my brain, shooting the wounded. I groaned and struggled to my feet, bumbling into the kitchen for anything liquid. Shielding my eyes from the savagery of the refrigerator light, I sucked down a half quart of orange juice.

"Are you ill, Gilby?"

I jumped, startling both Mother and myself. She looked at me suspiciously while a stream of orange juice flooded the sulky creases of my mouth and meandered down my chin. I imagined what I looked like from the expression on her face: sunken bloody eyes, imprint of seat cushions on cheek, Alfalfa hairdo. Gilby *Lost Weekend* Henderson.

She brushed off a kitchen chair and settled into it, alarmingly alert and fresh and, I was willing to bet, itching to drive that heaving Lincoln. I considered begging for this not to happen for a moment, but had to wait for a swell of nausea to subside.

"Gilby are you all right? You look like you just got back from the waterfront. Honest to mercy." She knew damn well I was hungover.

"I stayed up late and fell asleep on the couch," I said, avoiding her face and scanning the kitchen, first at the shelf of preserved jams no one would dare eat, the refrigerator with the "Keep Duke Mayor" bumper sticker, and near the utility room door, a hanging collage of laminated telephone numbers Sharon made when she was in the throes of what she called "Info Art."

I looked into my mother's eyes for the first time since reading the letters to Arthur Mirren. She exuded a sense of self-esteem, a sureness in everything she did, always there in front of you but never flaunting anything. You came away with the notion that she was never ashamed to be proud of herself.

"You're not listening," she said.

I could feel my hair sticking up in punk spikes and tried to mat it down with my hand before I became impaled on the ceiling. More than disappointment, much more than the surprise, I felt robbed of the perception of our history together. It was as though a piece of *my* life had been revealed and violated under the graceful strokes of her letters. The whole notion of Mother with another man was too consuming. She was supposed to be the one rock in this papier mache Henderson empire. The final insult of these letters seemed to be that her liaisons came to roost in *my* heart like some twisted spiritual incest, not the useless one that lay cold and inert in Duke's chest.

". . . and probably is." She had said something I missed again and finally raised her voice at me.

"Gilby, aside from your persistent drug and alcohol abuse, are you taking some kind of foreign medication?"

She slid an empty cup toward me, motioning with the coffee pot. I nodded dumbly and when she poured, a few drops splashed and spotted the back of my hand. The hot twinges from those beads felt like partial penance.

"I was saying that I'd like to get over to Hasty's this morning and pick out a marker for your father." She breathed into her coffee, parting the rising steam with the bow of her chin. I looked at her and wondered about that face in the hands of Arthur Mirren. Her body.

"You want me to drive you?"

"No, dear. I said I want you to help me pick out Duke's headstone. There will be some driving involved, but *I* will be doing it."

We stared at each other across the Formica expanse of the kitchen table.

"I don't know anything about tombstones."

"Well, that will be fine because I don't know much about driving. And they are referred to as headstones. The manager, Mr. Ablondi, calls them headstones. He says it sounds more upbeat."

I took a tentative sip of the coffee. "You're mocking me, right?"

"Somewhat, I suppose. But you *do* look like an escapee from a clinic somewhere. You can look like a bohemian all you'd like in that apartment of yours, but while you're living here I'd just as soon you—well, you know what I mean, dear. Anyway, I think it will be a long while until we get our world back on its feet and I want to be very busy."

"You know, the driving thing, Ma, I don't think is such a great idea," I said, scalding the roof of my mouth on the coffee. More penance; I should be even soon. "I mean, I'm glad you want to learn, but don't you think you should go to a driving school or something?"

She settled her cup back onto the saucer, the clatter making me wince. "It's a wonderful idea. And I know you'll be a very patient teacher."

I stood and walked over to the sink to inhale a glass of

water. The sun peaked through a low layer of clouds, dividing the kitchen with a slice of light as if in support of Mother's wish. She tried to smile again, but there was such sadness behind it she abandoned the effort.

"Gilby, one final thing about this place. I'm not going to keep this house just for memories. I don't want to live in a museum. We'll have to see how things work out."

"What would you want to do?"

"Maybe sell it. I don't know." She looked past me to the window over my shoulder. "It's much too early to be making decisions."

The crows scattered, giving way to the playful dipping and diving of the chickadees and house sparrows. A blue jay arrived, muscling in at the feeder and clearing the smaller birds out with a shudder of its wings.

"Where would you go?" I asked.

The sun gave her face a bronze appearance and I could see a sparse tract of soft white hair along the line of her jaw. Outside, the chickadees perched on the stunted white pine and squawked at the jay. Mother left my question floating in the warming air of the kitchen.

"How about you give yourself a makeover and we restart the day?" she said. "I assume you're not working today?"

I turned away from the window, smoothing my hair down again.

"Today, this week, who knows? As soon as a few aspirin help bring my soul back, we'll get going," I said and we both chuckled.

5.

It's not as though I didn't work, I just wasn't steady about it. My entry into the art restoration field had been through a college bulletin board. I found reading the bulletin boards at Northeastern far more entertaining and educational than any of the textbooks we were forced to buy. One day I copied down the phone number of "Monsieur Granville," whose ad read, "Conservator's apprentice wanted. Old man needs young eyes. Possible janitorial duties as well." I soon learned the ad should have just read "Janitor."

Granville was an elderly Parisian—a master conservator—whose consistently poor business decisions and dumb bad luck deposited him into a tiny apartment in the Back Bay late in life. He opened a restoration studio in a three story walkup on Marlborough Street about a block down from the French Library. For the three years I was his apprentice, Granville appeared to live a thoroughly French existence; taking his lunch at the French coffee shop on Arlington Street, nodding off in wing-back chairs at the French Library, and late at night listening to a French-Canadian radio station.

"The Canadians take my language," he told me, "And run it over with their lawn mowers before speaking."

I put up with the janitorial duties for a while, then after a few weeks I started to gripe at odd moments, sighing heavily during long sieges of broom sweeping. There was just so much dirt to sweep up, and when my complaints increased to a daily litany, it still had no effect on the stone-eared Granville.

"Look," I finally said one day, "you pay me enough to learn a few things about restoration, but not enough to be a goddamned janitor." Then, with great flourish, I said, "Please, Monsieur Granville, I must trade my broom for a smaller brush!"

That made him smile—what passed as a smile for Granville—and had I known how infrequently he did that, I might have celebrated more. As it turned out, during my entire tenure with Granville, he only smiled once more.

It happened after he had spent the greater part of an afternoon berating me for what he thought was a sloppy job on a surface cleaning. I felt I knew enough about what kind of a job I did to defend myself. So I stubbornly disagreed and he shuffled over to the black light as though that was the eye of God and put the painting under it. The varnish had been seamlessly removed. He tilted the painting at every possible angle as though playing a hand-held pinball game. Then he handed me the painting and farted quietly, a dignified fart if you can imagine one. I took this to be as close to a sign of approval as I was likely to get.

"What do you like most about French people, Gilby?" he asked me then.

"Their ignorance of their arrogance," I said immediately, one of those rare moments in life when one is simultaneously clever and accurate. Granville's smile started unhurriedly in the deep ripples of flesh carved into the corners of his mouth. Then a slight movement reverberated across his lips, parting them first in a sneer and then, as the lower lip caught up to the action, at last the suggestion of mirth. It danced slowly at first on his mouth, then spread over his entire face the way the sun seems to refresh everything after a cloud passes by.

The whole process lasted only a few seconds until gravity came calling and all joy dissolved, all merriment disappeared, and his face collapsed, as though exhausted, back into the frowzy grimace Granville had worn for the last few decades of his life.

But how I treasured that smile, because in that moment, I felt validated as an apprentice and in some shady Freudian corner, maybe even affirmed as my own man. I started taking the business of conservation seriously. Well, seriously for me.

Under Granville's great clumsy teaching, I began to level the ground that would establish a footing for my reputation. And in the world of conservation, your reputation is *all* that matters.

Granville taught me great patience with my work. His own involvement was so singularly focused and submerged that I felt a sense of adventure watching his face hover over a tear in a green field or a water mark on a lemon sky. He would lean into the painting, so close his nose would be shadowed by the exorbitant stroke of an artist's knife.

And that great gray head of his.

When he worked, Granville wore glasses so thick they gave me lens-nausea looking into them. What was left of his 85 year old body—a clatter of bones and skin—would lean in more and then the old man seemed to disappear into the work. There were moments when I wouldn't have been floored to see Granville step into a nineteenth-century still life so he could shine the flowerpot better. When he emerged, you knew there was not a shiver from the hand of the artist that Granville hadn't felt himself.

But because Granville used up all his patience as conservator, he had none as a teacher. He could convey his thoughts easily enough, croaking with French epithets, but he was fidgety with instructions and easily angered over the slightest deviation from them. He fired me three times during my first year, hiring me back each time because, as he explained, "I could not locate another imbecile."

One afternoon, some five months into my association with him, Granville scuffed over to my corner of the studio with a small painting in his gnarled hands. He handed it to me without a word and walked back to his easel where he had been haunting an old Japanese paper drawing for the past two weeks, hollering out, "Merde!" every fifteen minutes.

I placed the painting on my work stand as though it had been framed with volatile explosives. It was early twentieth-century, an oil painting of an abandoned barn that had succumbed to time. The varnish had yellowed considerably and there was a small chink of paint that had fallen out of the lush trees in the background, as though jarred loose by the restless wings of a barn owl. I stood there staring at the painting like a father just handed his new-born child. For the next few days after Granville handed me that painting, it never left my mind or my easel.

My joy came in finding myself in a Granville time fold, descending into a painting's buttery root, spending days and weeks with my hand on its beating heart. It didn't happen with every project, but when it did I wielded a reverent power over those works. I could go into a painting and hack its jungles to shreds with my scalpel or smooth its rocky perils with a brush. I was the great force that walked its silent woods and could turn back an army with a cotton swab or mend the world with the swipe of a rag.

I knew now that what made Granville great was his ability to suspend his own personality as an artist during the process. Granville was devoid of ego when he toiled and would never allow his own interpretation to impose on the work clamped before him.

"You must try on the shoes of the artist," he told me. "Then you must walk home in them and not take them off when you go to bed in case you have to walk in your dreams." I'm pretty sure he read that somewhere because Granville was not prone to poetics, but I got the point.

I wonder how my life would have played out if Granville hadn't died six months later. I worked fast and quietly for him during those last months and learned as much as I could about chemistry and the volatility of solvents—the science of restoration. Nothing is ever just fun.

Granville died on a Friday night and I learned about it in the obituary pages of the *Boston Globe* on Monday morning, an hour before I was to leave for work. At first, when I saw his name in tiny letters on the page, I thought someone was playing a tasteless joke on me. But there he was, his life summed up in a perfunctory paragraph. He was buried in

Mt. Auburn Cemetery in Cambridge with an elderly niece, a red-nosed rent-a-clergy, and myself in attendance. Halfway through the service it occurred to me that I had no job.

The next day I went back to his studio to clear out my brushes and chemicals when the phone rang. It was the Pell Museum in Boston asking if I would be interested in joining a restoration team working on a nineteenth-century Courbet painting called, "The Grotto." Granville had recommended me two weeks before.

Those first few days at the Pell Museum were nerve-racking, and though my work held up under the pressure, I always felt like some disaster was the slip of a swab away. Not that I didn't appreciate the husky hand of Courbet in my face every day for weeks, nor the generous check that arrived every other week, but the bureaucracy was enormous: forms for every procedure, work diaries, a doting curator to soothe.

After the Courbet painting was fully restored, the director approached me about a permanent position in their conservation department. I declined, saying I'd been thinking about starting my own studio, then I asked him about Granville's association with the museum. The director chuckled and shook his head.

"That old bastard hated museum work," he said to me. "He was consulted on a Thomas Eakins painting one time and barred the whole restoration team from the room. Just as a consultant, mind you. That's why I was surprised he gave you such a high recommendation. He loathed the structure of museum work."

I realized then that Granville's concluding assignment was to show me I didn't want a museum job either. The question had never come up between us, but he had anticipated it and now my education was truly complete.

Now I work strictly as a free lancer, but get most of my business from a restorer in Framingham who farms most of his work out and then charges for his services as if a team of scientists worked on it. I have my own key to the place and a space in his shop, and that's about as permanent an arrangement as I can handle.

I go to Granville's grave occasionally and love the way the stone is changing year by year, hammered and caressed by New England weather. No restoration necessary.

6.

Duke kept his car in the garage because he liked it to shine, so when I was old enough to drive and have a car, I always wound up on the street. My bequest now seemed to be parking in the driveway.

Mother came out wrapped up in a dark winter coat that would have been appropriate for a widow's stone-buying venture had she not perched a mauve beret on her head with the long Blue Jay feather stabbed into the side, creating an almost dashing look.

"Why don't I back Duke's car out of the garage and then you and I can go up and down Walnut for a while. Get the feel of things, you know, slow and steady?"

She nodded. I moved my car out of the driveway and was halfway up the lawn toward the garage when the Lincoln surged out of the opened door and came rocketing past me, Mother's feathered hat just visible through the darkened driver's window. The car paused momentarily at the end of the driveway, trembling slightly, then jerked out onto Walnut Street and stopped, its exhaust pipe panting clouds of smoke.

The horn blew and then a rear window magically lowered.

"Dear, close your mouth and the garage door and let's come on now," her voice warbled from inside the car.

When I got into the Lincoln, it seemed bigger than our

living room and I fumbled immediately for the seat belt. We didn't go anywhere. I looked at Mother and she gave me a half-hearted toss of her head.

"I admit I'm not good at judging distance yet while I have to work these pedals. That's really what I want to concentrate on, so keep your eye out for any pointers. But that's just a matter of time until I get used to it. Don't get too critical."

I looked behind us, relieved to see Walnut Street was quiet. "Look," I said, sighing. "If you want to drive, drive. Wake me when we get to the Oyster Festival in Nova Scotia."

"You're a good man, Gilby, she said, patting my leg. "Now, I do want your criticism, but constructively so. Don't be panicky because it will make me nervous, too. If I'm not doing well, you can take over when we get to Route 9."

"Why don't we just stay on Walnut Street for a while?"

For an answer she yanked the gear lever into drive and kicked up a few small stones from the street, spitting them behind us as we bullied through the stop sign on Walnut and headed left up Oak Road in this lethal gas-driven living room.

Mother drove with the same pugnacity that had marked Duke's belligerent career behind the wheel. He used to cut people off with relish and delighted in turning every driving predicament into automotive competition. First into the rotary, first off the red light, first to go at a four-way stop. The streets of Albright had been Duke's *autobahn*, so I shouldn't have been surprised with Mother's aggressiveness after all the years of riding with him. God help anything that stepped out from between the parked cars.

"Mother, you must stop at those stop signs, they're not just suggestions. And use signals, please. And go slower, please."

"Use signals even when no one is around?"

"They say it's a good habit to get into." My feet instinctively sought their own brake pedal. "And, Mother," I said, hanging on to the elbow rest, while Reggie's Groceria blurred by, "You have to slow down. This car feels a little out of control."

"That may be because you're closer to the parked cars, Gilby. I understand they can seem to be going by faster than they really are." She reached over and patted my leg again, making me glance fearfully over at her. "But I'll slow down."

"And both hands on the wheel, please."

"Both hands on the wheel," she repeated. "You seem nervous, dear. I'm slowing down."

Too late. Neither of us saw the police car until we heard it whooping behind us.

"You have to pull over now," I said, looking into the side mirror.

"I know that, Gilby. For God's sake, I watch TV."

A young Albright policemen walked up to the car and tapped at Mother's window. She pressed a button that lowered my window. This made her laugh. He waited patiently, his collar up against the harsh breeze. Then the back window on the driver's side went down. Now they both laughed.

"Well, you're on the right side of the car now, anyway," the cop said, smiling through the rear window.

Mother's window finally went down. "How are you, officer?" she asked.

"Oh, Mrs. Henderson, I'm fine, thanks." He quickly looked uncomfortable. "Ah, well, I guess I just wanted to express my sympathy. About the mayor and all."

"Thank you. Did you know my husband well?"

He put his hands in his jacket pockets. "Not real well. Mostly by reputation. A good one, though. A *real good* reputation." He took his hands out and blew on them. "Actually, Mrs. Henderson, I didn't realize it was you until I called the car in. Just kind of watch the speed and the stop signs, OK? And some signals, maybe? I wouldn't want you to get a ticket." He giggled nervously.

"Thank you," Mother said. "That's just what my son was saying to me."

He leaned over to look at me and tipped his hat. It was a polite gesture that looked ridiculous coming from a twenty-five-year-old baby face in a somber blue coat.

As soon as the police car headed up Oak Road, we were off again. Route 9 was mercifully only a couple more miles away and I would insist on a pilot change. Mother settled down to a more comfortable clip, but nothing you'd call sluggish.

I knew we were not going to stop when the gas pumps at the Mobil station whistled by and we banked out onto Route 9. She did better in this traffic though my heart pounded whenever anyone switched lanes in front of us. The speed she maintained in downtown Albright was the same one she used on Route 9 so at least it gave the illusion of being slower. And it was a much straighter line.

Hasty's Monuments had been in business in Albright for all of this century and a couple decades into the last, now tucked behind a paper-strewn alley in back of the Albright Patriot Mall. The only way in or out of Hasty's was on a single lane service road generously gouged with ruts.

"Hang on, Mother, I think you missed a pothole back there," I said.

"Sarcasm on a middle aged man is unattractive," she answered, the feather on her hat mashing against the roof of the car as we bounced along.

"Please go slower. And I don't see why we can't go to Framingham and do business with people who don't require four wheel drive to get to them," I said, bouncing exaggeratedly.

"Stop sounding like a grump, please. The family has done business with Hasty's for generations, Gilby. You know that. Duke liked to keep the money in Albright."

"It just makes me uncomfortable, buying a tombstone

from someone who wears nose jewelry."

"I told you, it's headstone. And what do you care what's in his nose as long as it isn't his finger? Alfred Ablondi is a perfectly nice young man. Honestly, Gilby, you sound like an old fuddy duddy."

We skidded up to the low gray building where several blank headstones were piled in front. Mother barely waited for the car to stop, then yanked on the door handle and stepped out onto the crushed stone drive. A head of dark hair emerged from the front door of the building, then the figure straightened and flashed a picket fence smile at us. Alfred Ablondi.

"Mrs. Hen'erson," he said. Must be in a new phase of expression because I didn't see any facial trinkets.

"Mr. Ablondi, how are you, sir?" She shook his hand.

"Extremely sorry we gotta see one another like this, ya know?"

How else would he see her? His personality aside, Ablondi's job made *no one* happy to see him. I offered my hand and mumbled, "Howya been, Alfred?"

"Chippin' away," he said while we shook. "And I just want to say you ain't goin' to replace Duke Hen'erson with no piece of granite. Am I right or wrong?"

"Marble," Mother said.

"Marble. Right, whatever," Ablondi said, wiping his hands on his shirt before offering Mother the escort of his dusty arm into the building.

We decided quickly on a simple marble stone, simple I say in terms of design, but the imposing grandiosity was all Duke. It was a five foot square block of off-white marble with veins running through it like the varicose rivers of an old map. I watched uncomfortably as Mother signed a check to Ablondi for God-knows-what in her sweeping hand.

Then she turned to me and said, "I'd like for you to come up with something for the stone, Gilby. Something Duke would have liked. An appropriate line or two."

Ablondi broke the silence by rattling some phlegm in his throat. I looked at Mother.

"You want what? Now? Right now?" I said. "You want me to come up with something off the cuff? For eternity?"

She looked over at Ablondi. "I don't want my name on there until I'm ready to use it, Mr. Ablondi."

"I catch your drift, Mrs. Hen'erson. It's bad luck I always felt. No sense in givin' providence any ideas. Am I right or wrong?"

"I'll be in the car, Gilby. Nothing melodramatic now."

"Mother, for God's sake, don't you think we should talk about this? Call Peter maybe? What do you want to say?"

She stopped and turned to look at me, gravel crunching under her shoes like old bones.

"I don't want to say anything, dear. There's nothing left unsaid between your father and me. This is for Duke, do you see? Mr. Ablondi has all the appropriate dates. You decide what you want him to put on it."

She walked back to the car and I felt a dreadful panic over coming up with something for Duke's stone, but not without the great relief of seeing my mother get in on the passenger's side. No more driving lessons today.

Ablondi handed me a pad and paper. "Make sure you get the words right. Spellin' ain't my specialty, ya know?"

I stood there looking at the darkened windows of Duke's car and for a brief moment imagined myself ensnared in some elaborate hoax, a cruel and complex practical joke masterminded by Duke himself. He was not dead but merely hiding in the wings, waiting to dash out from behind a curtain as if on Candid Camera, his barking laughter caroming off the headstones.

I stepped over a few polished slabs with familiar Albright names neatly etched on their faces—Stovall, Yurowitz, Bonetti, Duggins—the scope of entire lives abridged to a chiseled name and date. I set the pad and pencil on Duke's new stone and ran my hand along its cold intractable surface. It was a stone that seemed capable of mooring the earth, a fitting monument to Hizzoner.

I thought about Duke's actual death then, for the first time. About the pain composing itself ambiguously somewhere in his back or arm perhaps, then gaining impetus as it rumbled through his body, no longer a minor ache but now gaining his full attention. He must have said something to the girl he was with around that time. Or maybe she noticed his technique had changed. Then the wooden throb of it roiling into a tearing sensation until the whole medley of pain felt as though his chest had been ripped open and cold water thrown in.

Something to put on Duke's stone? Mayor. Lover. Friend. Husband. Father. Some of the above done well? Friend of the people? Somewhere from the dark mystery of memory an old quote started forming in my mind, and I could hear Duke saying it himself once, I just couldn't remember where. Something he bragged about stealing from an old Adlai Stevenson speech, one of Duke's big heroes. I toyed with it at first and knew I didn't have all the words exactly correct, but patiently and surely, as though Duke were whispering it slowly in my ear, it came to me. I wrote it out on the pad and handed it to Ablondi who looked at it as if it were in Sanskrit.

"The fuck's this mean?" he asked, squinting at the pad.

I looked at him with all the dignity I could muster. "It means just what it says, Alfred, *"Your public servants serve you right."*

We were quiet on the way home, and it felt as though we had both taken part in some finality with the headstone, but clearly we looked at it from different vantage points. Just before I was to turn at the Albright exit off Route 9, my mother wagged her finger toward the windshield.

"Keep going, Gilby," she said. "Let's go have lunch at the Salad Factory, shall we?"

As soon as we walked into the place, the owner, a painfully thin guy named Bernie who beat several drunk driving tickets thanks to my father, rushed over to us.

"Mrs. Henderson. Oh, we were all so sorry to hear about Duke," he said, and the cashier behind him nodded her agreement between ringing up checks. "He was a man who surely left his mark on this community."

The cashier nodded again and I wondered if Duke, as ubiquitous a swordsman in the sexual annals of Albright as ever there was, might have also left his mark on her.

"That's sweet of you, Bernie," my mother answered, taking his long bony hand in hers. Bernie looked like a cheeseburger might do him some good. "You remember my son, Gilby?"

"Of course," he said, but thankfully didn't offer me the same handshake.

Once we got settled, the idea of a Heineken didn't seem as reckless or imprudent as it might have an hour ago. Mother ordered a Waldorf salad with a Diet Coke and I went with the antipasto which was the unhealthiest thing I could find on the menu. When I asked for a Heineken, my mother's eyebrows went up one wrinkle, but when she didn't chide me for it, I knew she had something else on her mind.

"You want to get it out now, or wait until the tabouli and chick pea dessert?" I asked.

She smiled slightly and looked out the window at the cars racing by on Route 9. "You're a middle-aged man now, Gilby," she said. "And I don't like seeing you unhappy, but I'm starting to think that's just how it is."

I thought I might deny being unhappy, but she waved me off before I could utter a sound.

"I wish you had a loving wife and three chubby children.

I wish you had a passion for something that made everything else tedious. And I wish we were all twenty years younger so we could take another stab at it, but we can't."

The waitress arrived with our drinks and I tried not to chug the thing down but only half succeeded. "Driving lessons always made me thirsty," I said, hoping to lighten the moment.

"I'm going to break a promise I made to your father," she said. "It's not going to change how you feel, but I want you to think about it anyway. When Mr. Granville died and you came back to Albright, you went to work almost right away with Wayne Fitzpatrick over at Beaux Arts in Framingham, didn't you?"

I nodded, signaling for another beer. "Look, Ma, I know Duke put in the word for me, but once Fitz saw my work. . . ."

"Fitz realized right away that you were good at what you did. Put the word in? I'll tell you how Duke put the word in, Gilby, he bought Beaux Arts the day they buried Granville."

Now that was a surprise. Fitzpatrick and I had a pretty good working relationship, and he had told me Duke had been in to see him, but only to see if I could make a living. Fitzpatrick never let on that Duke had bought the place.

"Let me get this straight, am I supposed to feel good that Duke tried to pave my life? Jesus, Mother, that's even worse, isn't it?"

"Oh, Gilby, that's my point. It was such a microcosm of Duke," she said. "He just wanted you around so that maybe you two could try to be closer. That's all it was, but in Duke's grandiose way, of course. Doesn't intention count for anything?"

I was still too damaged from the night before to try to piece all the ramifications of this into the jigsaw of my life. And maybe that's why I didn't play fairly with Mother, but one revelation seemed to cry out for a partner.

"Now I'd like to ask you something," I said, smiling.

"How long did you see Arthur Mirren behind Duke's back?"

It seemed to be an afternoon for surprises. Mother looked at me for a few moments without saying anything, while the waitress brought my second beer along with our salads. Then she started to laugh. She laughed heartily, loudly, and for a long time. It was so infectious, I laughed with her, and there we were yukking it up at a corner table of the Salad Factory as though Duke hadn't died, but just gone into Jiffy Lube to get an oil change.

But we weren't laughing at the same thing.

"Gilby," my mother said, when she had composed herself. "Do you know who Arthur Mirren is?"

I was still ready to laugh, but just shook my head.

"Of course not, dear. He doesn't exist, never did. I made him up."

"What do you mean, you made him up?"

"I made him up. I wrote those letters to an imaginary lover and made damn sure your father found them in the filing cabinet."

I nearly swallowed my artichoke. "You wrote them to yourself?"

I'd never seen that look on my mother's face before. It was not what you'd call motherly, more that of just another passenger on the inexorable Duke train that ran through Albright. In that moment I was no longer the worrisome son, the other brother, the divorce statistic. My ticket was as valid as anyone else's.

"I wrote those letters, Gilby, because I didn't want to be the only one in the family without a secret," she said finally.

The Salad Factory was beginning to thin out, with many of the lunch trade headed back into Albright. Several people waved at Mother and she acknowledged them with a nod of her head. When she turned back her face was as radiant as I'd ever remembered, as though she had just returned from a lingering espresso with Arthur Mirren. I knew then that whatever my perception of my father had been and would be, beyond the backhands, insults, and misunderstandings, she had been the major component that kept it all from tragedy.

And it was Duke's final irony that she was his greatest act of grandiosity.

Acknowledgments

My sincere gratitude to the great teachers, writers, and friends I've been fortunate to have in my life, among them: Thomas E. Kennedy, James Carroll, Norman Mailer, Andre Dubus III, Art Devine, Dave Poe, Chris Tilghman, Pete Frawley, Mike Burns, Eric Miller, Pam Painter, Lexa Marshall, Gordon Weaver, Gladys Swan, Jim Gabriel, Anne Waterbury, Dan McCullough, Bob Sabbag, and Sven Birkerts. Thanks to my friends and talented colleagues at *The Cape Cod Voice,* especially Seth Rolbein for his unwavering faith and friendship. To the memory of Richard Duggins, and to two great influences that I sorely miss every day: Robie Macauley and Eddie Bonetti.

My thanks also to the Thursday cut and slash group—Dennis Cunningham, Pat Selmer, Laurie Higgins, Edie Sweet, and Beth Seiser for their keen eyes, insight, and fearless candor. Beth can keep secrets too. To Ira Wood for his relentless belief and saintly treatment. To Jean Naggar, for being much more than a literary agent. To the bad boys: Randy, Chad, Jeff, Mike, and Tim. To George Ryan, for a lifetime of lies, laughter, and friendship. To all my former writing students who have no idea how much they taught me.

And finally for Sarah, my love and gratitude always for the unexpected.

About the Author

Michael Lee is a Senior Editor at *The Cape Cod Voice* and a former editor of *Miami Magazine*. He received his MFA from Emerson College and lives on Cape Cod.

About the Type

This book is set in ITC Giovanni Book. The ITC Giovanni typeface was designed by Robert Slimbach and released by the International Typeface Corporation in 1989. Beginning at the drawing board and then moving to a computer, Slimbach based his design on classic oldstyle typefaces such as Garamond and Bembo.

Designed and composed by JTC Imagineering, Santa Maria, CA.